STAGECOACH TO HELL!

Austin Higby waited until the coaches were just twenty yards apart and thundering toward each other. Suddenly, he pulled hard on the lines and sent the lead horses into a sharp turn. The wheel horses tried to follow, but the Concord coach went into a skid and hit the exact rock that Higby had aimed for. The oaken spokes of the right back wheel shattered, and the Concord crashed over on its side with the sickening sound of splintering wood and twisting metal.

Jessie cried out as she felt herself being hurled into the sky. Beside her, Ki was launched off the stagecoach, too. He heard a tremendous crack as the Concord coach broke apart.

A scream filled the air...

WESLEY ELLIS

LONE STAR

AND THE
STAGECOACH WAR

A JOVE BOOK

LONE STAR AND THE STAGECOACH WAR

A Jove Book published by arrangement with
the author

PRINTING HISTORY
Jove edition/January 1987

ISBN: 0-515-08839-0

Jove Books are published by the Berkley Publishing Group,
200 Madison Avenue, New York, N.Y. 10016. The words
"A JOVE BOOK" and the "J" with sunburst are trademarks
belonging to Jove Publications, Inc.

PRINTED IN THE UNITED STATES OF AMERICA

Chapter 1

Jessica Starbuck and Ki walked purposefully through San Francisco's teeming Chinatown. It was a bright, sunny day, and in the distance they could see the Pacific Ocean dotted with sailing ships and fishing boats. The salty taste of the sea was as sharp as the fragrance of Chinese herbs and spices that bubbled in cooking pots. The streets were packed with vendors selling everything from incense to plucked chickens and Chinese fans. Down near the waterfront, raucous swarms of gulls fought noisily around the wharves, seeking the offal of the day's catch. As Jessie and Ki walked along, they attracted considerable attention from the rough European and American seamen who came in search of the delicate Chinese prostitutes who peddled opium as well as their bodies.

Jessie never failed to catch the eye, because she was tall, lithe, and lovely. The sea breeze riffled her long, copper-colored hair and made it sparkle in the sun. Jessie was in her twenties, long-legged with high, full breasts that accentuated her narrow waist. She greatly preferred to wear tight denim jeans and a wrangler jacket, but today she had an important business meeting with the Starbuck people about her shipping enterprises and had dressed conservatively. Because of this, no one mistook her for one of the white prostitutes who occasionally dared to enter the rougher sections of Chinatown in hopes of attracting the eye of a wealthy Oriental street merchant. One look at Jessie and the men who watched knew that here was a lady born and bred of high station, and one who could take care of herself and satisfy any man.

The older Chinese with hands strained by the opium pipe and inscrutable faces wrinkled like dried prunes paid particular attention to Ki. They knew at once that he was not even a little Chinese, for his eyes were too round, his cheeks too full, and his shoulders and body much too large. They correctly judged Ki to be half Japanese, half Caucasian. The Chinese hated the Japanese, for they had once invaded and conquered their mainland and were therefore considered to be enemies and a heathen people little more refined than the whites. But though they were heathen, the Japanese were feared and respected, and Ki had the look of a man skilled in the martial arts. The old Chinese looked away and the younger ones grudgingly stepped aside.

"They don't like you, do they?" Jessie asked, noticing the unfriendly looks thrown in Ki's direction and how the younger men faintly challenged him before stepping aside.

"No," Ki answered, "they will never forgive my mother's people for invading their lands. The idea of a small island people conquering the ancient armies of China is unthinkable to them, and yet it did happen. I understand their dislike. Once, I tried to explain to a Chinaman who spoke English that such historical things do not matter in this country and time. He refused to listen and we parted badly. He told me that all Chinese will forever distrust and dislike all Japanese. I fear this is the truth, for I remember how my samurai teacher, Hirata, spoke of the hatred of the Chinese. Yet he taught me something of their ways of fighting and thinking."

Jessie glanced sideways at Ki. He was not a good deal taller than she was, and yet she had seen him demolish men almost twice his weight simply by the use of his lethal hands and feet. In a time and country where most white

2

men looked upon anyone even half Oriental with unconcealed disgust, Ki was always greatly underestimated and often forced to defend his manhood. He had never failed to emerge victorious from such confrontations, and many was the time he had saved Jessie's life from men who thought a rich young woman was also easy prey.

They were now deep into the roughest section of Chinatown, and Jessie saw hard-looking groups of Chinese men staring at them. "We shouldn't have come this way," she said.

"We'll soon be out of here. Besides, it was the shortest route to your meeting," Ki said with a slight shrug of his broad shoulders. He was a handsome man, clean-shaven except for a thin mustache. His hair was black and longish and he wore a braided leather headband to keep it in place. His clothes were of the western style but, unlike most westerners, Ki wore no hat and preferred soft rope sandals to heavy boots. Ki moved with more natural grace than any man Jessie had ever known. He was as smooth-muscled as a cat and every bit as quick and dangerous.

"I know that," she said impatiently. Jessie carried a shoulder purse and inside of it was a gun that, when absolutely necessary, she could use as effectively as a riverboat gambler. "I just had forgotten how tough this neighborhood was."

Ki was thinking the same thing, although he did not want to admit it to Jessie and unduly alarm her. Had it been nighttime, they would already have been set upon by one of the tongs of Chinatown that murdered with ruthless efficiency. In daytime, however, there was some safety if they kept moving fast and stayed close to the center of the crowded street and away from the narrow, cluttered alleys where opium users and murderers lurked in wait.

Ki felt the presence of danger before he saw it. They still had two short blocks to go when suddenly, the street cleared and ahead of them stood three exceptionally large men dressed completely in black. These were not the thin, sallow-faced youths who had been watching them up to

3

now, but chosen tong assassins who ruled the streets of Chinatown. Ki touched Jessie's arm and stepped in front of her as the street people melted into the background.

Jessie slipped her hand inside her purse and started to pull out her gun, but Ki said, "If you open fire, they'll have friends who will do the same. We're surrounded, and the best thing we can do is keep walking forward, hit them hard and fast, then keep moving."

"All right," Jessie said, eyeing the huge tong warriors who stood like three blocks of stone in their path, "but I still think that . . ."

Her words died in her mouth as one of the Chinamen snarled, "Far enough! You givee money, nicee easy."

Ki lifted his hands palms up and smiled disarmingly. "I have no money," he said, still moving toward the three menacing figures.

"She havee money, you givee now!"

"I'll give you all I can," Ki said, moving forward so suddenly that he caught the big Chinaman standing flat-footed with a sweep lotus that caught the tong warrior in the throat and broke his larynx, dropping him strangling to his knees.

The other two men drew long swords but, before they were halfway drawn, Ki attacked with cold efficiency. The edge of his hand was like a blade as he used its iron-hard muscles to smash a second Chinaman across the side of the jaw and send him reeling. The third assassin did manage to get his killing sword out and take a swipe at Ki, but he was able to leap back out of the way enough to avoid the singing steel.

"Start moving," Ki hissed to Jessie as he and the Chinese tong warrior began to circle each other warily. "Once you go, don't look back and don't stop running!"

"Like hell I will," Jessie said, her green eyes scanning the crowd of Chinese who watched. She was searching for others who would interfere once Ki disabled the last Chinaman. "Just finish him off and let's get out of here!"

The deadly sword swished again with such suddenness

4

that it was merely a silver blur to the eye. "I'm trying," Ki said between clenched teeth as he feinted a foot strike that drew another sword swing.

Ki pretended to lose his balance for a moment and the Chinaman leapt forward with his killing sword lifted high for the finishing blow. Jessie's breath caught in her throat for an instant as she herself was fooled. But as the sword came down, Ki moved with incredible swiftness and came in under the Chinaman's powerful arms. Ki used a brutal knife-hand punch that landed just under the warrior's chin and lifted him completely off the ground. He then drove his stiffened fingers to the man's solar plexus, and Jessie saw the blood drain from the larger man's face. Ki finished the assassin off with a hip throw that smashed his opponent down to the street and knocked him unconscious.

A vicious snarl spun Jessie around just as the second assassin recovered enough to hurl a knife at Ki. "Look out!" she cried.

Ki dropped to the earth and the knife whistled past his ear. When the Chinaman reached into his loose-fitting black outfit and pulled a gun, Jessie beat him to the draw and her own weapon bucked in her fist. The Chinaman's shoulder erupted with a crimson blossom and the man screamed and fled.

"Let's get out of here!" Ki yelled as he leapt to his feet and grabbed Jessie.

Jessie wasn't about to argue. She held Ki's hand and together they darted up the narrow street, scattering Chinese in their path. Once, a rapid popping sound not unlike Chinese firecrackers swept the street behind them. But Jessie knew they weren't firecrackers when she saw a piece of wood splinter off a vendor's wagon.

A few breathless moments later they were out of Chinatown and striding up a steep hill into San Francisco's financial district, where bankers and businessmen awaited the daughter of Alex Starbuck.

At the huge stone entrance to the Bank of San Francisco, they halted to catch their breath and straighten their clothing. Jessie arranged her hair with a comb made of ivory and said, "Do I look presentable?"

"Yes," Ki answered, brushing a single errant tendril of her hair back into place. "Every inch the daughter of Alex Starbuck."

"Good." His answer pleased her very much, because the bankers she was about to meet with had revered her father. Alex Starbuck was a legend in San Francisco as well as around the world. His far-flung enterprises straddled the globe, but it was here he had gotten his start selling secondhand merchandise and a few well-chosen articles of real value that he had bought in the Far East.

Alex Starbuck had possessed a genius for making money and his import business had blossomed overnight. He had soon purchased a battered ship to carry trade goods from Japan and China to the United States. Ownership of another seagoing vessel quickly followed and then more. Other shipping lines had tried to crush the new upstart, but Alex had demonstrated a ruthless ability and determination to protect his own interests. Soon he had operated an entire fleet of trading vessels. Not satisfied with the work of other shipbuilders, Alex Starbuck had become a shipbuilder without peer and had been one of the first innovators to switch from the rotting wood hulls to those made of steel.

Steel was the future and Alex had bought mines in many parts of the world and then mills to refine it into the stuff that would make his merchant fleets the finest sailing any sea. The man had branched into many other enterprises. His steel had helped build locomotives and thousands of miles of railroad track. Soon, Alex was helping design better train engines and buying stock in America's railroads. As his empire grew, the need for ready cash had sent him into the banking business. He had helped establish the Bank of San Francisco and covered its early, formative years with his wealth, power, and prestige. He bought and sold real estate, dabbled in South American diamond mines, and helped finance democracies friendly to private enterprise. When he had died, it had taken accountants two years to get an idea of the amount of the Starbuck wealth. After the figures had climbed over ten million dollars, Jessie had lost count.

Like her father, Jessie's real love was the Circle Star Ranch in Texas, but she had inherited Alex's flair and financial ability. She had kept control over his empire with an efficiency that belied the rumors that she was just beautiful. The men she was about to meet with respected not only her power and wealth but also her ability, and she was proud of that. Jessie liked to deal with men on an equal footing in both the boardrooms of America's greatest companies and the bedrooms of cabins and palaces. Unconventional, sure. But just being a woman with so much power and influence was unconventional, so none of it mattered to her except trying to be the best, like her father had been before he was murdered by a vicious cartel that she and Ki had since smashed. Alex Starbuck was gone, but powerful bankers like those inside who awaited her would never forget the Starbuck name and legend.

The Bank of San Francisco was opulent and reflected both the Forty-Niner gold rush and the huge wealth that still flowed westward from the Comstock Lode in Nevada. The floors were solid marble and the wood counters and railings were of carved and polished teak and mahogany. Each of the bank officers had magnificent oak desks with plush swivel chairs. All eyes turned to Jessie and Ki when they entered. A young man who had been stationed specifically to greet her rushed forward with an outstretched hand.

"Miss Starbuck, what a pleasure to see you again after such a long time! How long has it been?"

"About six months, Norman."

"At least that long. Texas's gain is California's loss." He turned to Ki and greeted him with almost as much respect, because he knew how important the martial-arts master was to Jessie. "Ki, you've never looked more fit."

Ki just smiled and said nothing. He knew that he was being flattered because of his boss, and that had it not been for Jessie, he would not even have been allowed into the bank, which discouraged having working-class men and Orientals for customers. Someday that would probably change, but at present the Bank of San Francisco was very discriminating in its choice of clientele.

As Jessie shook hands with Norman Tibbett, one of the junior officers of the bank, she thought what a nice smile he had and how perfect a goodwill ambassador he was for this bank. Being one of the principal stockholders of the Bank of San Francisco, Jessie appreciated how effective a handsome young man could be in attracting the wealth of admiring widows. Some people thought that a widow who had been left with a large inheritance would prefer to deal with a bunch of graybeards, but Jessie didn't believe it for a minute. A young man like Norman would charm the socks off the wealthy depositors her bank was always seeking.

"I hope we're not too late," Jessie said, moving past the man and heading for the conference room. "We ran into a slight obstruction—three of them, actually."

"Oh?"

"It's already history," Ki said as they entered the plush conference room and began to shake hands with the bank directors. As always, Jessie took a seat near the head of the table beside the bank president, Mr. Friendel. Ki took his place in a chair at the opposite end of the table where he was immediately forgotten. It was a carefully chosen seating arrangement that left Ki free to observe each director closely without being too obvious. Later, when they were alone, Jessie and Ki would compare notes and impressions, and often the results would be very enlightening.

"Now that we are all together," Mr. Friendel said, lightly rapping a gavel on the tabletop, "I think we can begin with an open discussion of our bank's investment strategies. Quite frankly, since Miss Starbuck's suggestion over a year ago about the opportunities available to us in the Asian market, we have reaped an annual return of nearly twenty-five percent on our depositors' investments."

"That's wonderful!" one of the more enthusiastic directors interrupted. "The best we've ever done! I say we ought to—"

"Please, Mr. Gomper," Friendel blurted with obvious irritation, "let me finish my opening remarks."

"Sorry, Mr. Friendel."

"Now," the bank president continued somewhat stuffily, "as I was going to say, by continuing to use the Starbuck fleet of ships and by carefully monitoring our capital investments, I see no need whatsoever to alter our investment strategy and fully expect that—"

The door to the conference room burst open, much to Friendel's consternation, and Norman Tibbett stuck his head inside, obviously with great reluctance. "Excuse me, Mr. Friendel, but we have rather an emergency out here!"

"What kind of emergency?" Friendel said with complete exasperation.

"There is a Mr. Daniel Bonaday out in the lobby and he insists that he must see Miss Jessica Starbuck right this minute."

"Do you know the man, Miss Starbuck?"

"No."

Friendel looked pleased as he turned triumphantly to Tibbett and barked, "Tell this Bonaday fellow that an interruption right now is totally out of the question. Instruct the gentleman that he will have to wait until this afternoon when we have finished our business meeting. And don't interrupt us for any reason again!"

Jessie's eyebrows arched questioningly as she looked down the table at Ki, who shrugged to indicate that the name of Daniel Bonaday meant nothing to him either.

"Now then, before I was so rudely interrupted," Friendel continued, "I was saying that Miss Starbuck's father Alex, who used to be the president of this board of directors and a friend to us all, has left us with the option of renewing the lease of his ships for the Asian trade. Quite honestly, we are the real beneficiaries of his generosity, which is currently being manifested through the office of his heir and beloved daughter, Miss Jessica Starbuck. And unless any of you have contrary opinions, which I cannot imagine, I move that we renew the Starbuck leases and reward our stockholders with a dividend of—"

"Excuse me!" roared a big-shouldered man who burst into the room with Norman hanging on his coattails. Jessie saw that the intruder was in his early sixties but still possessed great power. He had wild gray hair and a ruddy face that showed the effects of a lot of hard wear and brawling.

"What is the meaning of this outrage?" Friendel cried. "Norman, evict this intruder at once!"

Norman tried to grab the man's thick forearm and paid for the effort by getting slung halfway across the room.

"I'll have my say with Miss Starbuck, by God!" the big man roared. "And none of you stuffed-shirted penguins are going to stop me!"

Ki rose from his chair as the intruder pushed inside. Almost unnoticed, he slipped down toward Jessie, ready to jump forward and protect her should this loud newcomer be addled of mind or in any way dangerous.

Jessie stood up and studied the man. She thought she had seen his face in a daguerrotype somewhere. "Mr. Daniel Bonaday. Have we met before?"

The big man leaned forward with his knuckles folded on the table. He stared at her so intently that Jessie did start to wonder if the man was demented or drunk.

"Yeah," he said after a long time, "we have, but you were only two years old at the time. I saved your life, Miss Starbuck. But I don't expect you to believe it and I have no proof to back my words."

Friendel rapped on the table. "Mr. Bonaday, this is very interesting, but would you mind—"

"Shut up, penguin," Bonaday rumbled ominously, his eyes never leaving Jessie's face. "I just came all the way back from Texas seeking this young lady and I'll not wait another moment to have a conversation with her. I demand to be heard."

10

Ki stepped closer. He seemed totally relaxed, yet Jessie knew that this was when he was most dangerous. "Sir, you do not demand anything of Miss Starbuck."

Bonaday threw a contemptuous backhand at Ki. If it had connected, it would have sent the much lighter man crashing against the wall. But Ki merely ducked the blow, and when Bonaday's wrist passed over his head, he grabbed it and twisted back and up. Bonaday was thrown across the table facedown, with his arm bent up between his shoulder blades.

"Let go of me, damn you!"

Ki held firm with no apparent effort. "Sir," he repeated, "I must ask you to treat a lady as she deserves to be treated. If you have a request, you may state it, but you do not demand anything."

"All right! I'll ask. Now let me loose!"

Jessie nodded and Ki stepped back, hands up, ready to parry a charge or blow. Jessie looked around the room at the directors, who appeared shaken by this unexpected turn of events.

"Gentlemen," she said, "in view of Mr. Bonaday's urgency and the excellent arrangement we have between us, I suggest you vote to continue leasing ships from my fleet and I will renew the lease at the same price and terms as before. Is this agreeable?"

Friendel nodded vigorously and his was the signal that sent all their heads to wagging in acceptance of the deal.

"Good," Jessie said. "Now, if you will excuse us and close the door behind you, Ki and I will get to the bottom of this pressing matter that sent Mr. Bonaday all the way to my Circle Star Ranch in Texas. Good day, gentlemen."

They were not used to being dismissed so summarily, and Jessie would not have done it under less pressing circumstances. When the door had closed, Jessie turned her attention to the agitated man who stood glaring at Ki as he rubbed his twisted arm. "I don't know how the deuce you did that, Chinaman, but I wouldn't try it again."

11

"He is not a Chinaman!" Jessie said hotly. "Ki is half Japanese and half American, and it was not by accident that you found yourself facedown and immobilized. Ki is my friend, and if you want to deal with me you'll deal with him as an equal, or I'll have him pitch you out of this room on your ear!"

Bonaday was taken aback by her anger. "Whoa there," he said. "I can see that I've ruffled your feathers and made a big mistake. But that's the story of my life."

Jessie relaxed. "You said that you had once saved my life. Tell me the circumstances."

"All right. It was right here in San Francisco and you were just two years old. I know that because you were taken out by a nanny to do some birthday-party shopping. Your father was tied up with some business and so he asked me to escort you and your nanny about town. I was happy to oblige because I owed Alex more than I could ever repay. You see, I once had a couple of ships myself, but they were destroyed in a typhoon off the Japans. All but one. I tried to compete against your father and the others but I didn't have the financial backing anymore. My credit was destroyed and I was almost bankrupt. Your father took care of that and got me back on my feet again. Later on, I sold out to him and he paid me more than what I had was worth. He was my friend. Best one I ever knew."

"I see." Jessie frowned. "You still haven't told me anything about how you saved my life."

"There's not a lot to tell. As we was going down Market Street, some men who recognized the nanny as being employed by Mr. Starbuck got the fine idea of kidnapping you for a ransom. They tried, and I killed three of them and took a bullet in the arm for doing so. Your nanny was not so fortunate and was killed instantly."

Jessie's eyes dropped to the floor. "That much is true. Her name was Mildred. I don't remember her, of course. But my father was quite upset and still spoke of her years later."

"She was a fine woman. She stepped in front of the baby buggy to shield you from harm, and when one of the men tried to grab you, she gave her life stopping him. She also gave me an extra second or two to settle the matter."

Bonaday rolled up his left sleeve to reveal a scar that still looked angry and ran from his wrist halfway to his elbow. "Shattered the bone, but I figured it was a small price to save Alex Starbuck's only child. I'd do it all over again in the same way."

"Is there anyone who will verify your story?"

Bonaday thought it over for a long moment. "Mr. Friendel's father will if he is still alive."

Jessie knew the banker's father and that he was alive. "I'll check on it. Assuming you are telling us the truth, how can I return that long-ago debt owed by my father?"

"Money. I need money."

Jessie sighed. Of course—she should have guessed.

"But not as a gift," he added quickly. "Hell, no! And when you get right to the honest heart of things, you don't owe me even a loan. Like I said, I owed your father everything when it happened. The score is dead even."

"How much money do you need, Mr. Bonaday? And for what purpose?"

"I need about thirty thousand dollars to keep my stage line operating until I can stand on my own two feet again. I have to be able to stay in business long enough to beat the men that are trying to ruin me."

"Where is your stage line?" Jessie knew that stage lines all over the West were going broke or being replaced by railroads.

"It runs between Reno, Nevada and Bishop, California, down along the eastern slope of the Sierra Nevadas. I service all the small farming and mining towns up and down the eastern slope. Used to be damned profitable until they started sabotaging my coaches and stations—driving off my horses and robbing the ore shipments. Doesn't take too many lost shipments of bullion to ruin a man."

13

"Who is doing it?" Ki asked.

Bonaday turned to include them both. "It's hard to say exactly. If it was just one or two men, I'd have killed them long ago and faced the consequences. But it ain't. It's a whole damn conspiracy that's out to ruin me and my family. I got a son that's been shot at and a daughter that don't have enough sense to know who's a friend or an enemy. I need money and I need help. And I needed it yesterday."

Bonaday took a deep breath. "They started their own stagecoach line in competition with mine. They're offering discount rates that are below the break-even point, but even that I can stand awhile. What I can't take is the way folks are losing confidence in my company. They get robbed and they switch stage lines in a hurry."

"Hire more shotgun guards," Jessie said.

"I tried that. They either buy them off or scare them off. Either way, I can't get men to ride my stages anymore."

Jessie glanced at Ki. "Why don't you go pay Mr. Friendel's father a nice visit?" she asked him. "When you get back, we can all decide what to do next."

Bonaday smiled. "So you're not going to take my word for it, huh?"

"It pays to check the facts, Mr. Bonaday."

"That's the girl!" He chuckled. "Now you're talking like Alex Starbuck's daughter. He was careful, too, your father was. He'd have checked my story out the same as you will. And when he discovered I was telling the truth, he'd have done anything he could to help."

Jessie nodded. "And so will I, Mr. Bonaday. So will I."

The man grinned hopefully. "That's what I figured from the very beginning, Miss Starbuck. I was betting everything I have left—which is damned little—that you had the same kind of character as your father. I reckon we'll be leaving for Reno tomorrow, huh?"

Jessie watched Ki pass quickly through the lobby. She had a hunch that the senior Mr. Friendel would substantiate Bonaday's story right down to the smallest detail. She and

14

Ki had not intended to go to work so soon and had even talked about taking a trip to the beautiful and refreshing Sandwich Islands. Now it looked as if they might be heading into the teeth of a storm over in Reno.

Funny, Jessie decided it sounded a whole lot more interesting anyway.

Chapter 2

Ki sat in the parlor of Mr. Adderly Friendel's two-story mansion while the butler went to inform the elderly man of his arrival. The room was richly furnished with Oriental jade carvings and oil paintings that Ki was sure had been a gift of the late Alex Starbuck. Until the elder Mr. Friendel's retirement as president of the Bank of San Francisco, he had been one of the most powerful financial figures on the West Coast. Alex Starbuck and Adderly Friendel had been close friends and had enjoyed years of mutually profitable business that had left the Friendel family among the richest in the city. Ki had met Adderly Friendel once before and remembered him as being a man who wasted little time on small talk.

"Ki," the ex-banker whispered as he appeared in the doorway. "Good to see you after so many years."

Ki arose from the overstuffed chair and was barely able to hide his shock, because the last time they had met, Friendel had been in good health. Now, however, the elder man was stooped over a cane and his face was gray with an unhealthy yellowish cast. Friendel hobbled forward and when he extended his hand, it was thin and without strength. Ki looked into the pain-filled, watery eyes of a man he knew was in his last year of life.

"It's good to see you too, sir. It's been seven years."

"Eight," Friendel said decisively enough to leave no doubt that at least his mental facilities were still in good working order. "It was the last time I saw Alex Starbuck alive. The bastards finally got to him, didn't they."

"Yes. We all miss him."

"There will never be another man his equal. Alex was a financial genius. He did things instinctively and I never knew his instincts to fail him. A genius in the truest sense of capitalism."

Friendel coughed and his body was racked by spasms. When he recovered, he had to be helped into an easy chair by his butler before he spoke again. "I hear that his daughter, Jessica, is all that he would have wanted her to be."

"She is, sir."

"Sit down, Ki. Can I have the butler bring us something to drink?"

"No, thank you."

Friendel nodded to his butler. "Ernest, two large brandies. If Ki does not drink his, I will see to it myself that it does not go to waste. Cuts the pain of old age, you know."

Ki nodded. He had known at first glance that something was eating away the insides of Adderly Friendel, and the deep lines of pain in the man's wasted face merely confirmed this diagnosis.

"What can I do for you?" Friendel asked, gripping the arms of his chair as if he were afraid of toppling forward to the floor.

"Does the name Daniel Bonaday mean anything to you, sir?"

"Of course. He used to be quite prominent on Knob Hill. A small-time shipping magnate and a big-time gambler. That man went through one fortune after the next. Spent at least a couple of hundred thousand dollars on lawyers to get rid of a succession of grasping wives. Daniel Bonaday was a very colorful man."

"A good one?"

"Good?" Friendel repeated, his thin brows arching in a

18

question. "That depends on your definition of the word. He was brave and honest, if that is what you mean. He always paid his debts. When he left town, there were some who sighed relief and others who figured San Francisco had lost a real character."

Ki frowned. He had not wanted to reveal Bonaday's claims, but now it seemed he might have to. "Did he and Mr. Starbuck know each other well?"

"Damn right they did! Those two once got in a fistfight down on the wharf and there are still a few men who claim it was the greatest brawl they had ever seen in their lives. Those two fought for two solid hours! The donnybrook ended in a draw when they both went into the bay and Alex discovered that Daniel Bonaday couldn't swim a stroke. Bonaday was still fighting, though!"

"He must have been quite a man."

"You say 'must have been.' Is Bonaday dead too?"

"No. In fact," Ki continued, "he is the reason why I'm here. He needs help and claims that he once saved Jessie from being kidnapped. Is that true?"

"Sure is! Made the headlines of the papers. You might still be able to find copies in the newspaper archives if you search around."

"That won't be necessary. Miss Starbuck merely wanted me to confirm the story. I think we'll help him out of some difficulty he's having over in Nevada."

"Alex Starbuck would help him if he were still alive."

Friendel finished his first brandy and downed the second in one gulp. He smacked his thin, bloodless lips together and sighed contentedly. "When you see Bonaday again, tell him old Adderly Friendel says hello and that if he needs a little cash, he should come by and pay me a visit. My son is already rich and a man can't take his money with him. Tell old Bonaday that money can't buy health, and when that's gone, a man hasn't a damn thing any longer."

Ki stood up. "I'll tell him," he said. "And thank you for your time."

The sick old man nodded weakly. "Thanks for the excuse to have the second brandy. Cuts the pain, you know."

Ki nodded. "I know."

The next day, they caught a riverboat up to Sacramento and boarded the Central Pacific Railroad for the trip over Donner Pass and down into Reno.

"I'd rather take a damned coach any old day," Bonaday grumped, "but there aren't any lines running this way anymore."

"The train is faster," Jessie said.

"A coach is a more dependable way to travel," Bonaday argued. "If the locomotive's boiler blows up or even springs a leak, we could be stranded for days. But if one of the horses in a stage team breaks its leg, the other five horses will still carry you on through."

Jessie had no wish to argue the point. Bonaday was a stage-line operator and bound to be partial to the old Concord coaches and their slower way of travel. Having already done more traveling than most people did in an entire lifetime, Jessie had used both conveyances and would take a train anytime over a stagecoach. First-class railroad passengers like they were could be assured of warm and luxurious travel compartments as well as the freedom to dine elegantly. And it certainly broke the tedium to be able to move around freely. On a stage, you might be pressed into a coach with eight other passengers and a few mail sacks thrown in for good measure. Coaches were rough and dusty. However, Jessie thought it unwise to point out the deficiencies of stagecoach travel to Bonaday. Besides, his point had been well taken when he had stated that there were many routes that could never be serviced by a railroad due to the high costs and low financial returns. Many unwise railroad companies had built track into the latest boomtown only to find that, by the time the line was completed, the ore had run out and the town was being deserted. Out west, towns birthed and died faster than mosquitoes.

Jessie enjoyed the ride over the Sierras. She watched as the train pulled into the low western foothills and then began the very serious climb up through Auburn. A few hours later they passed through Bloomer Cut, where thousands of Chinese had blasted and chopped their way through a granite ridge. Jessie viewed with interest the little railroad stops called Butte and Cisco where more Chinese had died during the bitter winters of railroad construction. It occurred to her that her father's steel was under the train they rode, and that made her very proud. She remembered how, when she was a small girl, Alex Starbuck had often told her stories about the bravery of the Chinese who had replaced many striking Irishmen at this end of the line. There had been a lot of strife over that, and many men simply had not believed the small, thin Chinese could stand up to the brutally hard work. Those men had been proven very wrong. Many of the disgruntled strikers had gone over to the Union Pacific Railroad. Happier on flat land, they had belted down track westward out of Omaha, Nebraska, fighting the Sioux and Cheyenne across the northern plains. The transcontinental railroad had been one hell of a race and a great piece of history.

"Excuse me," Daniel Bonaday said, interrupting the silence, "but did you recognize those two men who were sitting three seats down and watching us?"

"No," Jessie said. "I've been too busy admiring the scenery. The higher we get, the more beautiful these mountains become. Were the men friends of yours?"

"Nope, but I thought maybe they knew you and Ki. They kept looking over this way."

"I saw them," Ki said. "And I noticed that, too. But you have to understand that Miss Starbuck attracts a lot of stares from young men."

"Yeah, I can see how she would," the stage-line operator conceded. "I guess that was it after all. I'll have to admit I am jumpy as hell and suspicious of everyone. I've had two attempts on my life in Nevada. My boy, he's had one."

"And you have no clues as to who is trying to kill you?"

"Sure I do. But no proof." Bonaday lit a fat cigar and puffed until the smoke was thick enough to sting Jessie's lovely green eyes. "No goddamn proof, Miss Starbuck. But it's the same ones that are competing against me for the right to service the other side of this here mountain range."

Ki cleared his throat. "Mr. Bonaday, would you be so kind as to remove yourself until you are finished with that cigar? The smoke is bothering Miss Starbuck."

"It is?" One look at Jessie told him that Ki was right. "Well, damn me anyway for being such a lout! Sure I'll step outside on the platform and finish my smoke. I used to smoke such good cigars that women loved the smell of them, but lately. . . ."

"Thank you," Jessie said, wishing the man would quit talking and move outside. His cigar smelled like burning buffalo chips.

It took a few minutes for the air to clear after Bonaday had gone, and Jessie was not above using a newspaper to fan the air briskly. "That's another advantage of trains over coaches. In a coach, a man addicted to bad cigars has nowhere else to go and smoke."

Ki agreed. He would have opened a window, but it was too cold outside, and the skies were lead-gray and threatening. It was February and though it had been a mild winter so far, there were still patches of snow on the ground at this elevation and no doubt a whole lot more up on Donner Pass.

"What do you think?" Jessie asked. "Is the man imagining things or do you really believe that someone is trying to kill him and his son?"

"I guess we'll soon find out," Ki answered. "The smartest thing to do is play it safe and assume their lives are in danger. If that proves untrue, then so much the better. It sounds to me as if his opposition is winning, and that means murder would be unnecessary."

"I agree. But we must watch him carefully. We owe him a great debt."

They each watched the mountain. They saw the snow patches become a solid blanket and then thicken as the locomotive worked brutishly hard to pull them ever higher toward the great Summit Tunnel where the Central Pacific and the Chinese had almost been defeated—would have been defeated if they had not dared to use nitroglycerine to speed up the blasting of their final tunnels over the top.

"I'd better go and see if Bonaday wants to join us for supper," Ki said. "He's had time to finish that cigar by now. Besides, he must be half frozen after this amount of time on the platform."

"I'll go ahead and meet you both in the dining car," Jessie said.

Ki moved down the aisle in the direction that Bonaday had taken. He was reaching for the door of the coach when he happened to look through the grimy glass and see two men trying to lift Bonaday's inert form and preparing to throw him headlong off the train.

"Stop!" Ki shouted as he slammed outside into a buffeting wind. He had no choice but to lunge for the unconscious Bonaday, and that gave the pair the opportunity they needed to chop him with their gun barrels.

Ki grunted with pain. The platform was ice-cold and slick. Bonaday was hanging over a low guardrail, almost ready to topple onto the tracks where he might even be run over by the train. Ki felt hands beating at his head. One man managed to get his thick, powerful fingers around Ki's neck and started choking the life out of him. Ki knew that he could not hang onto Bonaday and have any chance of survival. He released the unconscious stage-line operator and gave him a desperate shove in hopes that he could at least send Bonaday flying far enough away from the train that he would not be cut in half by the wheels.

Ki was on both knees and his head was exploding with pain. But now his hands were free and he bent his fingers to his palms. With the last of his strength, he drove his rigid knuckles up and into his closer assailant's testicles. The man screamed in agony. Ki looked up to see the second man reversing his pistol to fire. Ki lunged at the man's knees and sent him backpedaling wildly. One minute the man was fumbling with his weapon, the next he was bent halfway over the rail and fighting for his balance. Ki grabbed his knees and heaved upward. A scream erupted from the man's lips and then died as he tumbled over backward and dropped under the moving train.

The first man still held his ruined testicles in one hand but there was a knife in his other. He swept in on Ki, who felt the blade slice through his jacket and score across his ribs. Ki knew that he had no strength left. The earlier blows to his head had left him dizzy. He felt the powerful man jerk his knife back and set himself to deliver the killing thrust. Ki twisted at the very last instant and the knife tangled in his jacket.

The man's breath was foul and hot; it came in short bursts of steam that were swept away by the icy wind. "Goddamn you!" he roared, trying to tear his knife free.

Ki's hand slipped into his jacket and found his *tanto* blade. He pulled the thin but razor-sharp blade from its lacquered sheath and drove it between the man's ribs. The man's eyes bulged and he lifted to his toes. His mouth formed a circle and, with an incredible effort, he threw his weight against Ki and they both crashed over the railing and flew into space.

Ki felt the wind hammer his body. He stared downward, certain that he would fall under the train and be cut in half by the iron wheels. But instead, he and the man locked with him in mortal combat were sent spinning over the edge of a steep ravine. When they hit the mountainside, Ki instinctively rolled into a ball and let his body absorb the punishment, softened only by the heavy snowfall. He crashed down through brush until he struck a pine tree and almost lost consciousness. He heard the lonesome shriek of the train whistle as the locomotive entered Summit Tunnel near the top of Donner Pass. And then there was nothing but a chill, deadly silence.

Ki knew that if he did not force his battered body into motion, he would quickly freeze to death. He took some snow and scrubbed his face hard and that cleared his head. He managed to crawl to his feet and stand. When he looked up the slope, he saw that he had rolled almost fifty feet down the mountainside. Not more than a dozen yards away, he saw the still body of the man who had carried him over the railing. Ki trudged over to him through deep snow and rolled him onto his back. The man was one of those who had been studying them on the train. Otherwise, he was a complete stranger.

Ki searched the dead man's pockets and was not surprised that the assassin had carried nothing that could identify him. Ki removed the man's heavy leather jacket, which was large enough to slip over his own. There was also a pair of warm gloves stuffed in the pockets, along with a gun. Ki figured he could make use of both.

Without a backward glance, Ki began to climb the snowy mountainside. It was very steep and slippery, and for every step up, he slid a half step back. Even so, he was in such superb physical condition that he quickly reached the railroad tracks. Just a few yards east, the black hole of the tunnel swallowed the tracks. To the west and back down toward Sacramento, the tracks were already icing over again after having been thawed from the weight and friction of their eastbound train. Ki wanted to go east. There was a train station at Donner Summit and he could reach it before night fell and the temperature plunged to zero.

Instead, he turned back west toward Sacramento. He had to look for Daniel Bonaday on the slim hope that he had tossed the man far enough out from the railroad tracks to save his life. Bonaday had been unconscious and even though it had only been a minute or two between the time he had gone over the rail and Ki's own sudden fall, the distance would be nearly a mile. Ki stepped onto the tracks and forced himself into a run. He ran lightly, but even so each stride brought jabs of pain into the center of his battered head.

He found Bonaday lying faceup in a snowbank. The man was breathing, but his pulse was rapid and shallow and his skin was ice-cold and marble-white. Ki dragged him onto the tracks and laid him out across the railroad ties. He removed the assassin's leather coat and covered the old stage-line operator before he dashed into the woods and began to gather up the driest firewood he could find. Ki was going to build a hugh bonfire right on the tracks. Sooner or later, either another train would come upon them, or Jessie would find a way to get help.

Ki looked up at the sky. The tops of the pine trees were beginning to sway and the heavy stormclouds were rolling east. The weather looked bad. More snow was coming and that was the last thing he needed. Ki knew that he would find a way to wait out and survive a blizzard, but he was not sure that old Bonaday would be strong enough to do the same.

One thing was for sure. If they ever got to Reno, he would never question the man's suspicions again.

Jessie was tired of waiting for Ki and Daniel Bonaday to join her. She had nearly memorized the railroad dining menu. All around her other passengers were eating scrumptious meals—veal, beef, roast chicken, and fresh fish.

"Excuse me," she said, getting up from her seat. "I'm going to go look for my lost companions."

The porter smiled. "Your table will be waiting when you are ready."

"Thank you."

Jessie hurried out of the dining car and back into the first-class coach. She had expected to see Ki and Bonaday and became concerned when she did not. Beckoning another porter, she said, "Have you seen the two gentlemen who were accompanying me?"

"No, ma'am," the colored porter said with a solemn shake of his head. "I thought they was in the dining room with you, Miz Starbuck."

"No, they weren't. Would you please help me find them? You search the train to the rear and I will go forward all the way to the coal tender if necessary."

It took a full half hour, but by the time the train had rolled to a standstill at the Donner Summit station, Jessie knew the awful truth. Ki and Daniel Bonaday were not on the train. She grabbed her heavy coat and a small valise and raced off the train into the station, which was little more than a small telegraph office. A potbellied stove was glowing cherry-red and the room seemed overheated after the outdoors cold. There were two heavily bundled men sitting on bare wooden benches near the stove. They had packs and they watched her with interest as she slammed the door behind her and strode toward the counter.

"We have to stop the train and go back," she said quickly. "There are at least two passengers missing—friends of mine. And I think there are two more men missing as well."

The telegraph operator, who doubled as a stationmaster, laid down a tattered copy of a month-old San Francisco newspaper. "I'm sorry, ma'am, but the train can't go back. There's another train coming through in four hours. The eastbound you just got off has to be off the track on a Reno siding or the next train can't get past."

"I don't care about that! There are four men out there somewhere. They can't be more than ten or fifteen miles back. We have to find them."

"I'm sorry. Couldn't stop the train even if I wanted to. There's a storm a-comin' and we need to get the eastbound passengers off this mountain. We send the train back, we might get it stuck. Risk a lot of lives. Can't be done."

Jessie wanted to scream in frustration. She understood that she was whipped and she had not thought about how her request might endanger everyone's lives. It was not uncommon for trains to get bogged down in Sierra blizzards or even knocked off the tracks during a sudden avalanche.

"The temperature is falling," she said. "I can't wait four hours. It might be too late by then. And it will be dark."

"Sorry, ma'am, but there ain't a thing I can do to help you."

Jessie spun around, hands knotted in her pockets. There had to be some way to get back down the tracks. "Do you have one of those handcars that you use to repair the tracks?"

"Sure, it's on the siding. But it takes two strong men to work it and I sure ain't going out in this weather. Besides, I got to stay here and operate the telegraph."

Jessie spun around and studied the two men sitting on the benches. "Are you men willing to help?"

They exchanged unenthusiastic glances. "We just want to get on the damn train and down to the Sacramento Valley where it's warm, ma'am."

"But you heard me! There are two men, maybe four, just west of here who need help!"

"Not our problem," said the other man. They were both full-bearded and looked to be in their thirties and very likely brothers. "Like the stationman said, it's mighty damn cold and windy out there. A fella could freeze on one of them damn little handcars. Sorry."

"Damnit!" Jessie choked. "All three of you disgust me! Never mind, it's downhill and I'll do it myself!"

"Hey, now wait a minute, lady, that there handcar is the property of the Central Pacific Railroad! You can't take it."

"Try and stop me, mister!" Jessie yelled, slamming the door and lowering her head to step out into the wind.

She found the handcar and had to scrape two feet of snow off it before she could climb on top. Jessie grabbed the handle and tried to push it down, but the handcar faced a very slight incline before it reached the main track and it must have weighed a thousand pounds.

"Uhh!" she grunted, jumping up on the handle and trying to bear down on it with all her weight.

The handle began to sink but the handcar barely moved. When Jessie had the handle as far down as it would go, she tried to lift it, and now her weight was of no advantage. The handcar was stuck and even though she strained until perspiration popped out across her forehead and froze like ice pellets, the car refused to budge. She wanted to cry, to scream, to tear into something or somebody. She lay gasping for breath, trying to decide what to do next.

"Aw, hell," one of the brothers said to the other as they stepped forward to help. "We ain't gentlemen but mama didn't raise us to be no-accounts either. Get off there, ma'am, and we'll see if we can get this damned thing to the main track for you."

"Thank you," she said gratefully. She had to be helped down, so weak was she after giving all her strength to the effort she had just undergone.

Even the brothers had to put their backs to the job and work to get the iron handcar to move up the slight incline. Once on the main track, however, they had to set its brake to keep it from rolling down the mountainside.

"Jake, can you image how fast this sucker would fly down to Sacramento? Be the ride of our lives, it would!"

"Otto, you mean you're a-thinkin' what I think you're a-thinkin'?"

"Sure! Hell, in four hours, we could be in Sacramento and save ourselves the fare to boot!"

"Now you're a-talkin'! Let's do 'er! Come on, lady, we'll take you for the most excitin' ride of your life!"

Jessie jumped on the car as they released the brake. The handles began to move up and down like a teeter-totter, faster and faster.

"Woowee!" Otto screamed. "Now this sucker is movin'!"

The brothers laughed mightily. Jessie just hugged the car and prayed that it would make the first curve they came upon without flying off the tracks. She peered ahead into

29

the gathering gloom. Their speed increased and her eyes began to water from the cold and wind. This was crazy, absolutely insane. But the brothers were right—it was the fastest and wildest ride of her life.

They shot through another tunnel out of absolute darkness into semidarkness. Jessie was numb. They had been screaming down the mountain at an unbelievable speed. The brake had busted loose and the handcar was totally out of control. Black shadows whipped past. Snow was falling and she was lying flat on the floor of the car, hanging on with her fingertips, legs, and toes. The brothers were no longer laughing with excitement. She could not see them clearly, only hear their screeches whenever the car lifted up on two wheels as it rounded another curve and they frantically shifted their weight to keep it from becoming airborne.

She saw a bright star like the sun. It grew larger and larger like a ball of fire as they raced down the mountain. Suddenly Jessie realized that they were hurtling straight for a huge fire. She screamed a warning and saw Ki drag a man off the tracks and leap for safety.

Jessie let go of the handcar and rolled. She felt her body lift and then smash into a deep snowbank. She heard a howl of pain and twisted to see the handcar with both brothers explode through the fire and be swallowed by the night. A moment later, she was being pulled out of the snow and Ki was shaking her.

"Jessie, are you all right?"

Not yet trusting her voice, she nodded.

Normally imperturbable, Ki was clearly shaken as he turned to stare at what had been his fire. Turning back to Jessie, his handsome face reflected shock and then a measure of wonder.

"Jessie," he said very seriously, "I think you should have just waited for the next train."

Chapter 3

They had waited until the westbound train came rumbling through and then they flagged it down. Because the train was on a fixed schedule, they had been forced to return to Sacramento, where they had immediately sought out a doctor to attend to the injured Bonaday.

"How is he?" Jessie asked when the doctor came out of the examining room.

"He'll be all right, but a couple of more blows to the head and he might have been finished." The doctor moved in closer to Ki. His fingers examined the knots and lacerations on Ki's scalp. "You could use a few stitches yourself, young man."

"No, thanks," Ki said, taking a step back.

"Suit yourself. I should tell you before I leave that Mr. Bonaday owes his life to his own thick skull and to your ability to keep him warm and dry. He was in shock, and that can be fatal to a man his age who is not cared for immediately. Do you know medicine?"

"A little," Ki admitted. "Mostly Oriental medicine."

"Oh, that," the doctor replied condescendingly. "Well, keep the man off his feet for a day or two and he should be fit to travel to Reno. I have given him some powders for a headache. If you want some as well, I can . . ."

Ki shook his head. The doctor shrugged and left them to

go inside and visit with Bonaday.

To Jessie, the stage-line owner looked far worse now than he had when she had seen him lying in the snow. His eyes were both purplish and there was a huge bandage around his head. It was obvious that he was in considerable pain, and yet he was anything but docile.

"Well," he demanded, looking at them belligerently, "do you two still think I've been making up stories about a group of men trying to ruin and kill me?"

Both Ki and Jessie shook their heads. "The problem," Jessie said pointedly, "is how to find out who's behind this and stop them."

"No identification on the man I found, one of the pair that tried to kill Mr. Bonaday," Ki said. "He was dead when I found him and couldn't help us by telling who paid for the job."

"Damn the luck!" Bonaday shouted, then winced from the pain he'd inflicted upon himself. "Sometimes I think that half the people in Reno are up against me. I know I've accused that many."

"Who is running the stage that is trying to put you out of business?"

"His name is Lee Ford. He's the senior honcho at the Sierra Stage Line. Ford is a short, fat, bald-headed sonofabitch with a waxed mustache that is redder than a baby's— well, it's mighty red. He and I have tangled two or three times, but since I know he's nothing more than a hired man, killin' him isn't worth getting hung for myself. I'm too damned wild to ever let anyone send me to prison."

Jessie shook her head. "We don't want either of those things to happen to you, Daniel. Somehow, we have to penetrate the conspiracy and find out who is behind the sabotage, robberies, and murder attempts."

"It'll be the folks who stand to gain the most money," Bonaday told them.

"Who owns the Sierra Stage Line?"

"Damned if I know. I tried to find out but was told it's a corporation and a lot of the money behind the operation is coming in from outside Nevada. But you can bet there are some local sharks swimming in that sewer as well."

"Then we must find out their identities," Jessie said. "And to have any chance of doing that, we have to create false identities for ourselves."

"I was thinking the same thing," Ki said. "If whoever is behind all this knew our purpose, we would never learn anything. What do you have in mind?"

Jessie had been thinking about it for the past hour or two. "We have to be people who have a reason to be involved with the Bonaday Stage Line, or at least have something to gain by either its success or failure."

"Maybe I could be Bonaday's old friend?" Ki suggested.

"You're much too young," Jessie said. She thought a moment longer, then added, "What if you were the son of a rich Oriental who lives in San Francisco? They know that Bonaday went there—why not to meet your father and seek a lifesaving infusion of money through a potential partnership?"

Ki nodded enthusiastically. "Yes, and that's why I'm so interested in learning all I can about the stage-line business. I need to advise my rich father."

"Exactly."

"Now wait a minute," Bonaday cautioned. "If they think that Ki and his imaginary Oriental father are going to invest in my company, won't they try to kill him?"

"That's the idea," Ki said quietly. "Or at least discourage me from thinking you have any chance of surviving their competing stage line. Either way, I will be a magnet for trouble."

Bonaday was not too happy with that and said so. "You might also get your head blown off, Ki."

Ki acknowledged this possibility with a smile. "We don't know who they are, so we have to bring them to us."

Jessie had complete faith in Ki's ability to take care of himself, but she wasn't about to allow him to take all the risks. "If you're going to play the rich young investor, then

33

I'm going to play the poor money-grasping relative."

Bonaday shook his head. "I don't have any relatives besides my two kids. Most of the time, I wish I didn't even have them."

"You have just acquired a niece," Jessie said. "Tell your son and daughter that I am the black sheep of the family. The girl born out of wedlock who went astray and is no damn good."

"You're too damn pretty to be bad."

"Some of the most beautiful women in history have been rotten to the core. It will work. I'll come to town without a penny to my name and be out to fleece you somehow of your money."

"How?"

"I don't know yet." Jessie smiled. "I'm hoping that your enemies will tell me."

"I better tell Roxy and Billy exactly what we are up to."

"No," Jessie said emphatically. "You've already said that your daughter doesn't know the difference between friends and enemies. We can't take the chance on her. Not until this is all over."

"You're right," Bonaday said reluctantly. "That girl is wild as a hare and whatever I want her to do, she goes ahead and does just the opposite to spite me."

Ki leaned forward. "What about your son? I imagine that I'll be working with him some. If his life is in danger, I want to be close at hand."

Bonaday smiled grimly. "Billy Bonaday is a man full growed and twenty-six years old. And I'll tell you another thing, if he ever thought for a single minute that some half-yellow, skinny fella like you was there to protect him, he'd blow higher than a damned volcano. Billy is tough as horseshoes and he backs down to nothing or nobody. He doesn't listen to anyone worth a damn, either. Stubborn, hot-tempered, always barging into what he don't know nothing about. Always chasin' pretty women—and catchin' them. Someday some husband is going to shoot his

—well, never mind that. You'll see what I mean when you meet him."

Jessie didn't like the sound of Bonaday's two offspring at all. From what she had heard so far, both Roxy and Billy were going to be far more trouble than help. That was too bad, because things were looking difficult enough without that kind of additional family complication.

Jessie stood up. "The doctor said you need to rest another day or two before traveling. Ki, you and Mr. Bonaday can take the train after the one that I'm going to take to Reno."

Ki could not hide his unhappiness at the plan. "I wish you would let us go first and then come a few days later. If anything happened and I was over here . . ."

"Nothing will happen," Jessie promised. "I'll just let it be known in town that I am looking for a way to fleece Mr. Bonaday. I'll say that he owed my mother a favor and I came to collect the debt. Maybe ask for some money or at least a good job. It will work. I'll also let it be known that I am bitter over the way that the Bonaday family ostracized my poor mother and treated her like she never existed."

Ki nodded. "You'll say you intend to get even with your uncle."

"Exactly."

Bonaday shook his head. "I still say you're just too damn beautiful a woman to convince anyone that you are no good. That, and you look . . ."

Jessie waited. She needed to hear what else was required to seem convincing in this unusual role of a down-and-out, grasping relative.

"I look what?"

"Too rich," Bonaday blurted. "Your clothes, your hair, everything about you smells of class and money."

Jessie laughed. "You should see me at the Circle Star Ranch during a roundup. I rope and brand cattle, work right beside my cowboys, and I can tell you that they wouldn't think I smell anything but bad out on the range!"

35

"Maybe so," Bonaday conceded, "but on your worst day a man would walk naked through an acre of cactus to saddle up with you in bed."

Jessie blushed. "You have a way with words, Mr. Bonaday."

"Hell," he said, "wait until you hear the sweet nothin's that jackass of a son of mine will whisper in your pretty, pink ear."

I can hardly wait, Jessie thought as she set about planning how she could look evil-hearted.

The train she took back over the Sierras almost didn't make it. An avalanche covered the tracks just east of Donner Pass and the train was delayed six hours. It happened twice more, despite their passing under miles of snowshed tunnels built into the slopes of the mountains just to prevent that sort of thing from happening. But at last, they were following the raging Truckee River into the high desert flatland to Reno. Jessie climbed off the train and all she had with her was a single, threadbare valise. She wore a man's workcoat and heavy woolen trousers and her shoes were broken and run-down at the heels. A slouch hat was pulled low over her brow and her lovely hair was bunched up in a knot under its crown. Unless a man looked closely, he would not even have guessed Jessie was a young woman, much less a rich, beautiful, and very shapely one.

"Where can I find the Bonaday Stage Line?" she asked a well-dressed business type who was probably waiting for some associate arriving by train from the coast.

"Down on South Virginia Street below the Truckee River about a half mile, mister . . . say, are you a woman?"

Jessie sneered and said boldly, "You got enough money, you can find out for yourself."

The man backed away as if she were poisonous. "Not interested," he said shortly. "But your kind can always scrape up a few fools willing to part with their money."

Jessie nodded. She had passed her first test and strode

36

off feeling as if her disguise and manner might just be convincing enough to serve her purpose. She headed down the street walking in long strides like a man, and even so it took her almost an hour to reach the stage-company offices.

When she entered, the place was nearly empty except for a few men lounging around the stove keeping warm. They gave her no more than a glance and went back to their conversation.

"Where can I find Daniel Bonaday?" she asked loudly.

The men stopped talking and stared at her, realizing she was a young woman. "What do you want to see him about?" one of the men asked.

"That's between Bonaday and me alone, mister."

"You want to buy a ticket and ride the stage south, I can sell it to you as well as he can."

"And who might you be?" Jessie asked, looking hard at the tall, rakishly handsome young man who was the spitting image of his father.

"Who's asking?"

"Vickie Wilson."

"That don't mean nothing to me. I'm Billy Bonaday and if you don't have the money to pay the fare, you might as well shuck it on out of here because—"

Jessie didn't let him finish. She pulled off her hat, shook her long, wavy hair loose, and let it fall to her shoulders. Bonaday had told her his son had a weakness for women; she was about to find out if that were true. "Because nothin', Billy. Don't you know who I am?"

She had caught him off-balance and she had no intention of letting him gain the upper hand now. "Hell, Billy, I am your long-lost cousin, Vickie! My mother and your father was brother and sister!"

Young Bonaday's mouth fell open. He closed it with a snap. "The hell you say! My father didn't have no sister!"

Jessie put an edge to her voice. "He tell you that all these years?"

37

Billy came forward and grabbed her by the arm. She slapped his hand away. "You keep your damn paws to yourself, cousin!"

"I ain't your cousin, I said!" He stepped forward to grab her again but when Jessie doubled up her fists, Billy decided that force was not the best way to handle her. "Listen, we can talk this out in my father's office. You need a few dollars or a free ticket outa this town, maybe we can work something out." He was looking at her body but she was dressed in such a heavy coat there was nothing worth seeing yet.

"I'll bet I know what that means," she said with a knowing wink that set all the other men in the office into snickering laughter.

"Shut up and get to work, all of you!" Billy roared in humiliation. "The stage to Carson leaves in an hour. And it had better be on time today!"

His employees shuffled off with smug grins.

"Damn worthless, the lot of them. If I was Pa, I'd fire every one or put a match under their behinds."

He waited until they had left the room and then he led the way into his father's office. It was a no-nonsense room with a big, rowel-scarred desk right in the center. A spittoon was overflowing with stubs of the same noxious cigars that Jessie remembered Bonaday smoking. There were papers scattered all over the desk and some harness that needed to be mended was piled in one corner. It did not look like the office of a profitable stage line.

Billy plunked himself into the desk chair and threw his long legs up onto the desk. He crossed them and studied Jessie closely. "All right," he said, "pull up your own chair and tell me who the hell you really are and what your game is."

Jessie sat down and dropped her hat to the floor. She looked right at the young man and said, "I really am your cousin Vickie and I came here to tell your pa that his sister died. I know my mother was the black sheep of the family and her name was never spoken because of that gambling man she ran away with in St. Louis. But she was his sister all the same as well as my mother. You and him are all the family I got, and I need help right now."

"Shoot," Billy hissed with disgust. "So you came all the way from St. Louis to Reno just to try and borrow some of my pa's money? Hell, girl, we're so poor I was about to ask you for a loan!"

Jessie stared at him with feigned disbelief. "Are you telling me the God's honest truth, Billy?"

"Hell yes, I am! Do you think I'd lie and say we was about bankrupt if we wasn't? Hell no, I wouldn't! Why, right this very minute my pa is in Texas or someplace else trying to talk someone out of some cash so we can meet the company payroll and keep the stages running on schedule. We are damn near busted, and if you don't believe it, go over and ask the sonsabitches at Sierra Stage Line who are driving us under!"

Jessie gnawed on her knuckles with pretended worry. "Damnit!" she swore. "I was hoping to get a stake here. At least a job!"

Billy shook his head sympathetically. "Honey, I couldn't pay you ten cents to shine my boots. We're that poor. As for a job, well, Pa and I have been laying off people instead of hiring them. I can't help you a lick and neither will Pa when he comes back—if he comes back."

"You mean your own pa might have skipped out and left you holding the bag?"

"Maybe. He would have if he was smart. But he ain't smart, so I expect he'll come draggin' back in here one of these days to preside over the corpse of this failed business."

Jessie snatched her hat off the floor and climbed to her feet. "No sense in my waiting around for the funeral."

"Not when you see the lay of things, Vickie."

She eyed him closely and hesitated at the door. "Even when a business goes under, there's usually some stuff that's auctioned off. That'd be worth plenty. Maybe I'll stick around a while longer in case that happens or you get this show in gear."

This decision did not please Billy. "You can wait until hell freezes over before you'll get a thing outa this company! And you'll have to stand in line behind everybody else we owe. If every horse, every damned coach and piece of harness this company owns was auctioned off tomorrow for debts, there wouldn't be enough left to buy a damned licorice stick. So why don't you get yourself outa here before I toss you out!"

Jessie stood up. "I think you're lying to me, Billy. You got a sister, don't you?"

"Yeah. So what?"

"What's her name?"

"What business is it to you?"

"She's my cousin!" Jessie stormed. "I got a right to at least know her name."

"Roxy," he said grudgingly. "But she ain't worth any more than you appear to be worth. Hell, she's even going out with some fella that I think owns some of the Sierra State Line. Can you believe that!"

"If he has money, why not?" Jessie tossed her head defiantly. "Money is all that matters. A man's good looks don't count for nothing but trouble. I'll take a rich, homely man any day over someone like you, Billy. I'm glad I found out right away that you ain't worth bothering with nohow."

"Get out of this office!" he yelled, dropping his feet to the floor and coming around the desk.

Jessie got out. She had accomplished what she had wanted to accomplish. Her acting had been better than she had hoped for and she was sure that Billy had believed her story completely. He had her pegged as a worthless, scheming relative who was no better than her mother had been. Billy would have to tell his men about her designs. And Jessie would just bet the story would get to the Sierra Stage Line during the next twenty-four hours. After that, she would pay them a visit and see if they were interested in giving her a break. People out to destroy a common foe usually found an advantage in working together.

Jessie stepped out into the street and looked both ways. She wanted a hotel and a bath but it would have to be a run-down establishment befitting her supposed economic distress. And she was hungry, too.

The hell with it, Jessie thought, trudging back into the main part of Reno. *I may have to settle for a fleabag hotel, but I'm going to eat steak while I'm doing it.*

Chapter 4

Jessie ate well, but her night in the low-class hotel room was turning out to be much less satisfactory. Afraid that she might not be able to pay her bill, the hotel clerk had taken it upon himself to send her up some revenue in the form of a couple of men looking for a real good time. It was after midnight and the men outside her door were very persistent.

"Listen," she said. "Go away! I am tired and I want to go to sleep!"

"Aw, c'mon, Vickie! We got a little bottle here and we are ready to celebrate. You can sleep any old night."

"Get lost, damnit!"

"We got money, Vickie! And we ain't cheap if you show us a real good time in bed. Ain't that right, Jim?"

The man named Jim belched loudly, then said, "That's right, Vickie, honey. Open up and we'll pay you five dollars each."

Jessie pressed her body against the locked door and cursed silently. Damn these two and double-damn the hotel clerk for giving them her name. "If you two don't get away from this door, I'll—"

"You'll what? Call the sheriff? Call the hotel clerk?" They began to laugh uproariously. "Lady, you might as well—"

"That ties it!" Jessie said, moving across her room to yank out the special pistol her father had given her on her eighteenth birthday. It was a custom-built Colt .38 on a .44-caliber frame. Jessie had gotten so good with it that she could squeeze off five rounds before most men could accurately fire three with their heavier weapons.

She returned to the door to find it bouncing back and forth against the frame as the two men outside threw their shoulders to the wood. She had to give this pair credit for their determination.

"This is your last warning, gents! Get lost or I open fire!"

But right at that very moment, the door broke free from its hinges and slammed down flat with the pair sprawled out on top of it. Jessie just managed to leap back out of the way and then the two men were climbing to their feet and trying not to spill their whiskey. Jessie fired twice without seeming to take aim. The bottle in each man's fist exploded in a shower of glass and liquor.

"Jesus Christ!" one of the men shrieked as he whirled for the gaping doorway. "She's got a gun and she's gonna kill us!"

The second man scrambled across the door, slipped, fell, and cut his hand badly on broken glass. He howled and then charged out of the room and down the hallway. The entire hotel shook when the two men tripped at the stair landing and tumbled down into the lobby.

Jessie scowled at the door and the mess. "The hell with it," she said, grabbing her pants and pulling them on before shrugging into her heavy coat. She grabbed her threadbare valise and stomped out of the room.

There were men standing in their doorways along the hall, some of them almost naked, but she paid them no attention as she marched to the stairs and down into the lobby.

"Miss Wilson!" the desk clerk shouted. "You can't just leave without making restitution for the damages!"

Jessie yanked her sixgun out of her purse and her first

44

bullet shattered a kerosene desk lamp. Her second ripped a furrow along the open desk register and slammed it into the man's chest. He cried out in fright and pain, but Jessie didn't even look back over her shoulder at the snake when she stalked out of the smelly old hotel. There was a good, clean place just up the street, but it was too expensive for a girl who was supposed to be down to her last few dollars. *The hell with it,* Jessie thought, *everyone has to draw the line somewhere.*

The next morning, Jessie thought things over and decided that she would have no hope at all of getting a job with the Sierra Stage Line dressed the way she was now. Besides, she was already sick of the baggy old clothes and the slouch hat. The thing to do, she decided, was to look lean and hungry, but good. With that in mind, she spent the rest of the morning buying herself a modest but appealing outfit. A couple of dresses, nice but inexpensive shoes, and a warm coat that was fashionable two years ago.

She threw out the hat and combed her hair until it shone. A green ribbon complimented her copperish hair and she even applied a touch of perfume. Standing before the mirror, she appraised herself carefully. Her clothes were quite modest but revealed enough of her lush figure to attract the attention of any man. Jessie wanted to go to work for Bonaday's competitor because it would give her access to the Sierra Stage Line's accounting system. If she had enough time to dig through the records, there was no doubt in her mind that she would discover who were the real powers behind the company. With any luck at all, perhaps she could also find out who was behind the assassination attempt that had almost succeeded in killing Bonaday up near Donner Pass. Jessie knew that it was vitally important to learn everything possible; not only was the old stage-line owner's life in grave jeopardy, but so was Ki's life when it became known that he was a potential investor who might be able to save the ailing Bonaday Stage Line.

Jessie slipped her gun into the purse she had bought at a

secondhand store. She left her hotel after asking directions to the Sierra Stage Line offices and moved purposefully down the street, aware once again of the admiring glances bestowed upon her. It was good to be desirable again. Maybe that was considered sinful by most clergy, but that didn't change the way a woman felt about herself. Especially a woman trying to look her best and out to trick some unsuspecting man like Lee Ford into giving her a job.

In contrast to the poor and seedy appearance of the Bonaday Stage Line offices, those of the Sierra Stage Line were new and prosperous-looking. They were right downtown and near the Truckee River Bridge. The stage line had purchased several acres of land and the stables for their horses were neat. Jessie saw three new stages being readied for service. The Concord coaches were things of beauty during the first few years after they were received from the factory. Jessie had once visited the famous manufacturer in Concord, New Hampshire, and had come away more than impressed by the craftsmanship used to make these coaches. Not only were they built with the finest materials available, but every single coach was individually decorated by artists. The coaches she now saw were red and sported magnificent gold scrollwork. Each door was painted with a small but classic landscape, and even the spokes were pin-striped and polished to a high sheen. The entire coach was coated with many layers of varnish and the effect was dazzling. Jessie knew these coaches had cost the Sierra Stage Line about two thousand dollars each, plus shipping. That said a lot about the amount of money that was being pumped into this company.

Jessie had nothing against competition, and if this company was better operated and financed, then she believed it should eventually drive a weaker competitor out of business. Alex Starbuck had been the ruin of hundreds of competitors in various markets around the world. Today, Jessie hired the best managers and businessmen she could get to see that Starbuck empire remained sound and competitive. Sometimes, the very size of her operations left smaller companies with the advantage of speedier decision-making and, when that happened, Jessie lost business. It was all a game, really. The strongest, most innovative, and hungriest businesses forced out the weaker. In that way, the free-enterprise system was self-regulating to ensure that the consumer always got the best service or product at the best price.

But what the Sierra Stage Line was doing was perverting the rules of competition. You didn't sabotage your opponent's operation, frighten off his employees, and rob his clients. That was not only unlawful, but against all the rules that business played by. Price-cutting and even loss-taking measures to drive a weaker opponent under were acceptable. Hired assassins and sabotage were not.

A low whistle from one of the stage-line employees caught the attention of his peers, and suddenly work stopped completely as Jessie admired the shiny, new coaches and the men admired Jessie. Aware that she was supposed to be a harder person than she was, and slightly naughty, Jessie waved at them and smiled. The men hooted and started toward her. Slightly unnerved by what little provocation it required to start a stampede of lusting man-hood, Jessie retreated out of the yard and into the company offices.

"Can I help you?" a smallish man who wore a pair of thick glasses and a cheap but clean and well-pressed suit asked.

Jessie correctly guessed him as an accountant, and therefore someone whose support she would like to cultivate. "Yes, thank you. I am looking for a Mr. Lee Ford. Is he in?"

"He's busy at the moment. Did you . . ." The man could not keep his myopic eyes from dropping to stare at the proud swell of Jessie's bosom. He swallowed nervously, a thin, frail sort in his early thirties whom Jessie noticed wore a wedding band on his bony finger. "Did you have an appointment, Miss . . .?"

"Wilson. Vickie Wilson," she said with a warm smile,

despite the fact that she was angry with this married man for his stupid gawking at her figure. "May I wait to see him?"

"Oh, yes," he almost whispered. "Can I get you a cup of coffee, Miss Wilson?"

"That would be nice. Thank you. Black is fine."

He dashed into another room and was back in a moment with a cup. When he presented it to her they touched, and he almost spilled the hot coffee all over himself. He looked faint.

Jessie took the coffee thinking that she would have to go very easy with this man. He looked all too frail and excitable to be able to take much flirting from her. He was the kind of fool who could get her into a corner if she were not extremely careful.

"My name is Peter Bakemore, Miss Wilson. I am the head accountant for the Sierra Stage Line." He smiled self-deprecatingly. "Actually, I am the only accountant."

"Then you must be a very important man."

He filled his narrow chest and bounced a little on the balls of his feet. "Well, it is quite a responsibility. I do need help, though. I am, quite frankly, overworked and underpaid."

"I'm sorry to hear that. My father was a businessman and I learned very early the importance of keeping good records. If the record system of a growing company is weak, the entire company will suffer. Don't you agree, Mr. Bakemore?"

"Absolutely! How I wish you could convince Mr. Ford of your words. He thinks that record-keeping is . . ."

"Superfluous?"

"Yes, exactly! How did you guess?"

Jessie shrugged modestly. "They don't understand people like us. Because we understand figures and they only understand the day-to-day operations, they mistrust us just a little. Being an accountant can be very lonely and unrewarding."

The man was beside himself with joy. "Miss Wilson,"

he breathed, "I can't tell you how much I appreciate your rare insight and understanding! You are a remarkable young lady. I would give anything if . . ."

"If what?"

He shook his head. "I was just fantasizing about how well we would work together. It would be so . . . so nice."

Jessie batted her eyelashes demurely. "As a matter of fact, I have come looking for employment, Mr. Bakemore. Though I dare not hope for something so lofty as to become your personal assistant."

"I need you!" he blurted. "And I will do everything in my power to influence Mr. Lee to hire you."

"Thank you," Jessie said with deep gratitude in her voice.

Bakemore was gazing into her eyes almost transfixed when a short, heavyset man in his twenties stomped into the room and bellowed, "Bakemore, goddamnit, what are you doin' moonin' over this woman when you are two weeks behind on the books!"

Bakemore jumped in fright. But to Jessie's surprise, he did summon up the nerve to hiss, "This is Miss Vickie Wilson and she is seeking employment. Her credentials in bookkeeping and records are impeccable. I think you should hire her on the spot, Mr. Ford. I need her!"

"Jesus Christ," the man growled. "She looks like she could do a whole lot better using her looks rather than her brains."

He waddled forward, a really obese man with a red face, bald head, and bulging chipmunk cheeks. His belly was enormous and hung far over his belt. His blue eyes were bloodshot, deep-set but very probing, and gave evidence of high intelligence. Jessie saw a native cunning in Ford that warned her she needed to be very careful indeed. This was not a man who could be easily charmed or deceived. Flirting with him was out of the question—Jessie knew with certainty that no woman had ever flirted with Lee Ford except to gain something. He was a very repulsive man.

"I ain't hiring no bookkeepers today," he grunted. "What else can you do for money?"

The insinuation was insulting and Jessie chose to ignore the question. "I think I can help your company destroy the Bonaday Stage Line," she said, looking right into those crafty little eyes. "Interested?"

"Maybe," he said after a long pause. "Come into my office, Miss . . .?"

"Wilson. Vickie Wilson."

"Yeah. Bring your coffee along. I want to hear your angle." His fat lips curled in disdain. "Bakemore, get your ass to the chair and start adding and subtracting your goddamn numbers!"

Bakemore jumped to work and began working so furiously that Jessie felt sorry for the pathetic little accountant. He certainly did need some help. She wondered how much he really knew about this company. Somehow, she thought that he was too delicate in nature to be trusted with knowledge that would imply wrongdoing. But he would know where the money was coming from and going to, and Jessie could find out the rest.

"Sit down," Ford ordered, squeezing behind his littered desk. The room was a pigsty and suited Ford perfectly.

"Now," the man said. "Tell me how the hell someone like you can help someone like me break Bonaday any faster than we already are."

Jessie had not expected to be confronted so directly. She had expected this meeting to be influenced by her womanhood, but now she could clearly see that was not going to be the case. It meant that she would have to use her intelligence against his, and she was prepared to do so without hesitation.

"I'm Bonaday's niece," she said. "I figure that he owes me something and I mean to collect."

"Shit," the man growled. "Do you know Bonaday is almost bankrupt?"

"Yes. His son told me that yesterday. He also said that

his father is seeking financial backing and may have found it."

Ford blinked. "Who the hell would help him? They'd have to be crazy given what the Bonaday Stage Line is up against right now. The man hasn't any credit!"

Jessie shrugged. "All I'm telling you is what my cousin, Billy Bonaday, told me yesterday. His father is in San Francisco and is seeking funds."

Ford leaned forward. "I knew that. We watch him carefully. But I've heard nothing about the man having any luck whatsoever. And even if he did have . . ."

Jessie saw the man smile and change his incriminating line of thought. She knew with dead certainty that he had almost said that, even if Bonaday did find help, he wouldn't have lived to return to Reno.

"And even if he did have," Ford continued, "it wouldn't matter. The man is already ruined and he doesn't know it yet. Besides, if you really are his niece, why aren't you over there trying to help the man?"

Jessie had anticipated this question. "He and the rest of the family never forgave my mother for having me illegitimately."

Ford blinked with surprise.

"Are you shocked at my candor?"

"Yeah, I am," he admitted. "It takes guts to admit you're a bastard. Or does that word just apply to *men* born without fathers?"

"It applies to either sex, Mr. Ford," she said coldly. "And is used most cruelly in any case."

Her anger had the desired effect. "I'm sorry," he said. "I just wanted to see how tough you really are. So you hate your uncle, huh?"

She nodded. "And after being thrown out of the Bonaday offices yesterday, I haven't much use for my handsome cousin."

"He threw you out?"

"He did."

51

"You must have really said something wrong. He's a womanizer. Someone like you . . . well, he would normally have tried to get you into the sack right away."

"I'm his cousin."

"You're a damned good-looking hunk of woman," Ford corrected. "Cousin or not, it wouldn't have made a damn bit of difference to Billy. His brains are all below his belt buckle."

Jessie said nothing. The assessment was probably true and there was no sense in denying it. Billy had an animal attraction about him and Jessie figured that most women would oblige him in any way he wanted.

"What did you do to make him so mad?"

"I asked for money or a job."

"So, you're down on your luck, is that it?"

"I'm not ready to hustle for money, if that's what you mean, Mr. Ford. But neither have I a savings account at the local bank."

He grinned with amusement and pulled a cigar out of his top desk drawer. He lit it and kept grinning as his lips sucked at the cigar and then formed his next words. "I like you, Vickie. You strike me as a no-bullshit broad. A woman who's hungry, but not desperate enough to be a whore. Tell me the truth, do you really know a damn thing about record-keeping, or was that all just smoke to impress Bakemore?"

"I know record-keeping," Jessie said. "Inside and outside. Frontward and backward."

"And you want to help us destroy Bonaday?"

"*Crush him,* Mr. Ford. Crush and humiliate the man for what he did to my poor dear mother, God rest her soul."

"Are you a woman who can keep her mouth shut?"

"Try me."

He stared at her as he would have at a shrewd competitor, not caring that she was also beautiful. "All right," he said finally. "I will."

Chapter 5

Ki and Daniel Bonaday were delayed for five days by the heavy snowstorms that pounded the Sierras. Seventeen miles of snowsheds collapsed under some of the largest avalanches in recorded history. The Central Pacific Railroad sent hundreds of men up to clear the tracks. Men in tandem with the huge snowplows pushed by teams of locomotives finally broke through the snow. The telegraph wires between Sacramento and Reno hummed with the good news that the trains could start running again on schedule.

That same morning, Lee Ford sent Jessie a message to come to his office at once. When she walked in, Peter Bakemore again rushed to greet her, but Ford was there to intercept her and usher her into his office.

"Something unexpected has taken place," he said, his small eyes studying her carefully. "I have not been able to reach two of my employees who should have been on the train that's due here this afternoon."

Jessie nodded. He was talking about the pair of assassins. No doubt he had been frantically trying to contact them to learn if there was any truth to the story that Jessie had given him about Bonaday getting financial help.

"How does their absence affect me, Mr. Ford?"

"I'm not sure. But let us suppose that, instead of my

men arriving as planned, off the train should step none other than Daniel Bonaday and a friend. A rich friend."

"All right. Suppose they do. So what?"

Lee Ford bent forward. "I want you to be at the train station to meet them—if they arrive. Try to learn as much as you can. If Bonaday really has been successful in attracting an investor—and one would have to be crazy to buy into his game—then I want to know as much about him as you can find out."

"You want me to spy on him?"

"Exactly," a voice said. It was followed by the appearance of a man Jessie had never seen before. He had been in the next office listening to them. He was tall, extremely good-looking, and in his early forties. His long black hair was edged with silver around his temples. He had dark eyes and a lush mustache. He was lean and athletic and possessed one of the finest smiles of any man Jessie had ever seen. He studied her very closely. "Are you willing to be our spy, Miss Vickie Wilson?"

She stood up. "Who are you?"

He extended his hand with an amused smile on his lips. "My name is Orin Grayson. Assemblyman Grayson. I'm in the state assembly, but I consider myself more of a businessman than a politician. It's an honor to meet you. Lee has told me you are quite a woman. I can see at a glance he has not exaggerated your . . . assets, Miss Wilson."

She felt heat rise in her cheeks as his eyes casually undressed her. "Thank you." Jessie took his hand and when he held it in his, she could almost feel an electricity in his touch.

The man had a powerful attraction. She wondered if he was the one behind the plot to ruin Bonaday. As a politician and businessman, he might be rich and influential enough to be the power behind the Sierra Stage Line.

"May I call you Vickie? You may call me Orin."

"Of course, Orin." Jessie pulled her hand away and smiled. "I'll be happy to meet my uncle if he is on the train, and then to tell you everything I can discover about his recent trip."

"That would be a big help." Orin frowned. "You see, Vickie, Mr. Bonaday is a very narrow-minded and opinionated man. I should tell you right now that he hates me and this company because we are more efficient and better run than his operation. Also, I have been seeing his daughter, Miss Roxy Bonaday, and he strongly disapproves."

Jessie nodded. She remembered now that Bonaday had mentioned that his headstrong young daughter was seeing a man he considered his enemy.

"Roxy and I are . . . well, little more than very good friends. She understands that business is business. I had hoped that she might influence her father to sell out to us before he is completely ruined. But I realize now he won't do that. Stubborn pride is the downfall of so many men. Better by far if he had sold out when he had the chance and reaped at least some small reward."

"Has Miss Bonaday tried to talk him into selling out to you?"

"Of course. Roxy is an intelligent girl. She can see the handwriting on the wall and doesn't want to see her father walk away with nothing."

"And what about the son, Billy?"

Orin and Lee Ford both scoffed. "Billy is a strutting peacock, a man who cares for very little except women, wine, and song. He plays a bad hand of poker and, though he does have a dangerously quick temper, he doesn't concern us in the least."

"Mr. Bonaday might not be willing to talk to me any more readily than his son. Especially if Billy tells him how he ran me off."

"Don't worry about Billy," Lee Ford said. "A very talented woman up in Room 205 of the Pine Tree Hotel will make sure that Billy doesn't know or even care that his father has finally returned."

"I see." Jessie nodded. "All right. I will try my best.

But I do want to know what I am to receive in return for this unusual request."

Lee Ford clapped his fat hands together in appreciation. "See, Orin!" he exclaimed proudly. "I told you she had her feet on the ground and her hand reaching for someone's pocket. The lady wants to know what we'll pay her."

Orin nodded. "I like to be very honest in my dealings with people," he said. "You have every right to know that you will be amply repaid for your trouble. If Daniel Bonaday is on that train and has a prospective investor, and if you help us by finding out all you can, then I will see that you are paid one hundred dollars tonight."

"One hundred dollars?" Jessie shook her head and acted immensely impressed. "Why, that's more than most accountants receive in two months."

Ford said, "It's more than Bakemore gets in three months, but I don't have to tell you that our dealings are hush-hush."

Orin nodded. "Yes. Poor Bakemore already feels underpaid and overworked. And he is! But the man is a weakling and hasn't the courage to demand what is fair. Somehow, Vickie, I have the feeling that you are a woman who will demand everything you have coming, and then some."

Jessie smiled. "You're right," she said sweetly. "Now, if you'll excuse me, I have to leave and get ready to meet that train."

Orin stepped aside just enough for her to squeeze past him into the hallway. "Vickie, why don't you come by here after dark and tell me what you have learned."

"But what if Mr. Bonaday isn't on the train."

"Come by anyway," Orin Grayson said. "In case something terrible should ever happen to Daniel Bonaday, we can discuss how you could best help us to break young Billy. For a woman like you, that would be as easy as taking candy from an overgrown baby."

Jessie nodded and slipped past them. On her way out of the Sierra Stage Line offices, the head accountant waved meekly to her and whispered, "I'm doing everything in my power to get you a position as my assistant, Miss Wilson. How did the interview go in there?"

Jessie thought for a moment about how she was expected to meet Orin Grayson tonight in this very office. "It is to be continued this evening," she said to the accountant.

He beamed. "Excellent! That's wonderful news. Mr. Grayson must have really been impressed with you."

"Yes," she said, her mind swirling as she left the room, "I think he was."

Jessie stood waiting at the station while the train ground to a ponderous halt. Jessie saw families eagerly awaiting to be reunited and, as always, it reminded her that, except for Ki, she really had no family. Many friends, yes, but she was the only living Starbuck. Someday, she might settle down and marry, have children, and begin to let someone else gradually assume control of the Starbuck empire. But she was in no hurry—she was still a young woman.

Jessie happened to turn around and see a man watching her. This confirmed her suspicion that either Orin Grayson or Lee Ford had sent someone to observe her meeting with Daniel Bonaday. They were supposed to be strangers, uncle and niece meeting for the very first time. If Bonaday displayed any familiarity with her, Jessie knew that her fabricated story would be shot full of holes.

But how was she to warn Ki or Bonaday not to betray her when they disembarked? Jessie saw a shoeshine boy and hurried over to him.

"Do you know Mr. Daniel Bonaday on sight?" she asked. "Big man with—"

"Sure I know him," the kid said. "He owns that old, run-down stage line."

"Better not say that to him." Jessie scribbled a quick, warning note to Bonaday that read: *You and Ki pretend we are strangers. JS.* Then she handed the note to the boy along with a dollar and sent him racing to the first-class coach, which was starting to unload.

The Sierra Stage Line spy betrayed no change in expression. Jessie knew she had outsmarted them. Supposedly having never met Bonaday, she would need someone like the shoeshine boy to seek him out, so the note had been a very natural tool to use. Ki, of course, would destroy it, and the two would be forewarned.

Bonaday stepped off the train first. His eyes searched for Jessie in the crowd. Ki appeared next and Jessie almost failed to recognize him. He was dressed in a very handsomely cut business suit with conventional shoes, a tie, and a stylish Stetson hat. His long black hair, however, was braided into a queue that hung down his back. No one would have suspected he was anything but exactly what he appeared to be: a rich young businessman of mixed Oriental and European ancestry.

Ki saw Jessie first, but his eyes flicked over her and displayed no recognition. Only Jessie could read the fleeting smile, the touch of relief and joy he felt at seeing her alive and well again.

The shoeshine boy waved and pointed at Bonaday, and Jessie moved forward through the throng of passengers and greeters to join him. The spy also pushed forward, but Jessie had too large a lead on the man and the first thing she whispered to Bonaday and Ki was, "We are being watched and closely followed. Help me get you where we can talk privately."

Ki nodded and his eyes instantly picked out the man who was shadowing Jessie. For a moment he considered *atemi,* the use of pressure points located primarily in the head, neck, and shoulder areas, by which a man skilled in their application could instantly render an opponent unconscious. But that would create more problems than it would solve. Ki scolded himself inwardly for forgetting that he was supposed to be a rich young businessman—a financial, but certainly not a physical threat to anyone.

Bonaday signaled one of the number of men and boys who operated buggies to earn a few dollars whenever a train arrived. They were lucky enough to get a surrey driven by a young man named Dusty who Bonaday knew quite well. "Dusty, help us grab up Mr. Chen Ling's and my baggage and then get us out of here."

"Where to? Your offices?"

"Yeah," Bonaday said, "at least that's the direction you can start off in."

"Yes, sir!"

A few minutes later they were in the surrey and heading up South Virginia Street. They said nothing until Jessie looked back and saw they had lost the man who had been shadowing them. Still, Jessie knew they could not talk freely with Dusty just an arm's length away.

Evidently the same thought occurred to Bonaday. "Why don't we get out and walk the rest of the way? Dusty, you go ahead and deliver our bags at my office," he said, giving the boy two nickels—all the money he had in his pockets.

Jessie shook her head to realize the man who had once owned a fleet of sailing ships was now completely broke. "Here, Dusty," she said, handing the boy two dollars. "And thanks for the help."

"Yes, ma'am! Thank you!"

He drove off then just as happy as could be.

They hopped out and strolled along the busy street. When they reached the Truckee River, they angled along the riverfront and found a private hiding place in the trees.

Jessie saw the man sent to shadow her go racing over the bridge looking about wildly for her, Bonaday, and Ki. "We can talk now." She touched Ki's cheek affectionately. "It's a relief to see you again."

"And you," he said. "I was worried, Jessie. Sitting around in Sacramento knowing that you were over here in the lions' den, so to speak, wasn't easy."

"I'm fine. I've even got a job with your competitor, Dan."

"Good work," the older man said roughly. "What have you found out so far?"

"Not much. Learning about you and Ki is really my first job."

Bonaday's mouth dropped open. "You mean we just got rid of two goddamn spies and you're another one?"

"Yes," Jessie answered defiantly. "But have you forgotten whose side I am really on?"

He toed the ground with his boot, then picked up a flat rock near the riverbank and sent it skipping across the water. "Six jumps! Goddamn it, used to be I never got less than seven. Age'll be the death of me if Billy and Roxy ain't first."

"Dan," Ki said patiently, "we haven't much time to talk. Come back here in the trees and let's find out what Jessie is up to."

Jessie explained everything that had happened from her first meeting with the Sierra Stage Line accountant to her meeting with Lee Ford and then Orin Grayson.

At the mention of the latter man's name, Bonaday flushed with anger. "That sonofabitch is damn near old enough to be Roxy's father! I should have shot him years ago."

"And gone to the gallows?" Jessie asked. "That wouldn't have been very smart. The man is a state assemblyman. You and the Bonaday line would have been crucified."

"Do you think he's the money behind them?" Ki asked.

"No," Jessie said pensively, "at least, not all of it. I'm hoping that I'll find out a lot more after seeing their books."

"They've gotta be losing a pile of money every single day," Bonaday said. "New coaches, new harness, and all that office space and prime land. They've cut prices so low that we lose on every mile we carry a passenger."

"Grayson told me he tried to buy you out."

"Yeah, at ten cents on the dollar. I told him and Lee Ford where to stick their offer. I'd rather go down fighting and have nothing than knuckle under meekly and crawl out of Reno. You know just as soon as I leave the Sierra Stage Line will double its fares. They'll make people wish to God they'd helped me keep some competition along these mountains. Anybody new tries to move in, they'll be burned and run out. Grayson, Ford, and whoever else he has behind him are going to bleed the people of Reno, Carson City, and the little towns all the way south to Bishop. Be a damn shame."

Ki asked, "Did you tell them about me?"

"I only hinted. I have to report to Grayson this evening on who you are and how much money you can pump into the Bonaday operation."

"What will you tell him?"

Jessie smiled. "That you're filthy rich and have money to deposit in the bank tomorrow."

"Good," Ki said. "That means that they'll try to rob or even kill me tonight. With any luck, maybe we can wrap this up early."

"You're going to have to be damn careful," Bonaday warned. "These people don't play to lose."

"Neither do I," Ki said quietly.

Bonaday nodded. "We better get on over to my office and see what kind of mess Billy is creating today. I swear that man is more trouble than he's worth sometimes."

"Billy might not be in this afternoon," Jessie said.

"Where the hell else would he be! Someone has to be in charge when I'm not there."

Jessie shrugged. It would do no good at all to tell Bonaday that his son's attentions had been distracted by a hired prostitute and that he was up in Room 205 of the Pine Tree Hotel. That would only serve to make the stage-line operator all the more disgusted and angry. Angry enough, perhaps, to say or do something about it. And that would cast a suspicious finger right at her.

Jessie reach out and touched Ki on the arm. "I'm going to try to find out what I can from Orin Grayson this evening. And I will have to tell him you're rich enough to get the Bonaday line on its feet and keep it there for a long, long time. I've even set up a line of credit at the bank for you to use."

Ki nodded with a smile. "We might have to use it today

61

just to get enough money to have dinner, right, Dan?"

"Damn right," the older man grunted. "You saw the empty bottoms of my pants pockets. My wallet ain't in any better shape."

"Well, it's a ten-thousand-dollar line. That can buy a lot of steak."

Bonaday whistled. "Is it ours to spend? I'm about two months behind on the payroll and if I don't return with money, the few men I got left will quit today."

"Pay them all," Jessie said. "We can't win if we aren't in the game. Pay all your bills and tell everyone in town that Mr. Ling here is your rich partner. There is nothing that will force the Sierra Stage Line into action faster."

"Starting with me tonight, I hope," Ki said.

Jessie nodded, but she was worried. She did not want to make any promises, but if it was humanly possible, she intended to be around when they came to pay Ki a visit.

Orin Grayson opened the door the moment she knocked. He was freshly shaven and smelled of bay rum. Once again, Jessie was struck by how attractive he was. It was her experience that men with a few years on them often made the best lovers. They were more experienced, slower to reach a climax, often possessing a little more tenderness and consideration than a man in his twenties.

"Come in, Vickie," he said, closing the door behind her quickly and escorting her into his office, where Lee Ford sat sipping a bottle of whiskey. "We were very disappointed to learn that Dan Bonaday returned, accompanied by a Chinese friend of some means."

Jessie replied with some annoyance, "I thought it was my job to find that out."

"Oh, it is," Grayson said quickly, as he poured two glasses of brandy from a crystal decanter and handed her one. It was a very expensive brand that her father had once loved and that Jessie enjoyed as well.

She raised her glass. "To success."

They toasted as well.

"Now," Jessie said. "The hundred dollars, please."

Grayson shook his head and winked. "Later. After you tell us the things we still don't know. You left in a surrey with Bonaday and his rich Chinaman friend. Then what happened?"

"They were hungry and stopped for something to eat. We talked privately."

"And?"

Jessie feigned anger. "My uncle didn't appreciate my asking for money any more than Billy did. He explained to me how things were, but then five seconds later he was bragging about how Mr. Chen Ling was a very smart man to invest in his company."

"Then the decision has already been made?"

Jessie hesitated. She decided to say no, for that would mean these men might only try to discourage rather than kill outright. "Not necessarily. I mean, I could tell that Chen Ling was the man with all the money. He even paid for the lunch!"

"I told you, Orin," Ford said. "Dan Bonaday is flat broke. He couldn't have lasted another day in Reno without losing everything. And now that his creditors know that he has some stupid Chinaman backing him up, they'll come flocking. I'll bet Bonaday owes five or ten grand to the merchants and his own employees."

Grayson's eyes were flint-hard. "Who cares if we almost had the man! He's got a sucker on his hook and one so rich we might never break him. A few of those San Francisco Chinamen are filthy rich! It's just our luck that Bonaday found one."

"Then we'll just have to show the Chink that not only is the Bonaday operation failing, but it's also very unhealthy."

"You didn't hear that Vickie." The state assemblyman finished his brandy and refilled their glasses. "How old are you?"

She looked him right in the eye. "Old enough to ask you again for that one hundred dollars I was promised. Old enough to take what I want from life when I get the chance."

He laughed and opened his desk drawer to pull out a miniature strongbox. From his watch chain, he produced a little gold key and opened the box. Then he extracted a hundred dollars and gave it to Jessie. "Do you have anything else to tell us?"

"Not tonight."

Grayson glanced sideways at Lee Ford. "Good night, Lee. Lock the front door on your way out."

Lee blinked. Jessie suddenly realized he was a little drunk, but not so much that he didn't quickly catch the meaning. "Sure, boss," he said, lurching his bulk out of the chair and grinning obscenely. "You lucky bastard you."

"Good night," Grayson repeated coldly. "Vickie and I still have a few details to work out before she comes to work here tomorrow."

"Yeah, sure. When she shows up in the morning, Bakemore ain't going to know up from down for about a week."

"I'll explain things to her about Bakemore. Now, get lost."

Ford licked his lips and headed for the door. When it had been closed and locked, Grayson pulled another hundred dollars out of his strongbox and laid it on the desktop. "You are a very lovely woman, Vickie. But somehow, I am still not convinced you are exactly who you say."

Jessie took a deep breath and stared at the money. "Are you trying to buy the truth with that hundred-dollar bill?"

"Of course not. Even if you were lying you'd be smart enough not to admit it at this point in the game. No, what has me puzzled is that you don't look hungry enough. You're staying in a nice hotel, not the kind of flophouse one would expect a girl who had no money would choose."

"I have a little money," Jessie said tightly. "But not much. I came to make some real money."

"Good," he said softly. "And now, I'm going to put those words to the test and give you the chance to prove what you say. If you're really hungry and out to use and destroy your uncle, you'll gladly undress right here and we'll have a good time on that big leather couch you're sitting on right now. But if you're not, then you'll refuse."

Jessie stood up. "I have never done it for money before, and I won't start now!"

He chuckled softly and put the hundred-dollar bill away. He locked the strongbox up and replaced it in his drawer. Then he came around to her, placed his hands on her shoulders, and drew her body to his own. Kissing her neck, he whispered, "I knew that you'd say that, Vickie. You're too ambitious to sell out for a lousy hundred dollars. But if you let me make love to you here and now, I promise you'll get more than you ever dreamed."

She felt herself shiver with anticipation. He smelled and felt good. It had been weeks since she had had a man and much longer since she'd had one like this. "Why don't you take me out to dinner and we can talk about it then?"

"I can't," he whispered. "You see, someone would tell Miss Bonaday and, until this is over, I need her to tell me how her father's day-to-day operation is running. She is very . . . very possessive."

Grayson stepped back and began to unbutton Jessie's dress. When he had it about halfway done, he reached inside under her thin chemise and smiled as he cupped one of her full breasts in his hand. Then he slipped the chemise off and lowered his head. Jessie gasped to feel his tongue begin to lick her swelling nipple. She arched her breasts forward and slipped her fingers into his hair to press him closer. "Why don't you tell me exactly what I stand to gain before we go any farther."

"A stage line. A monopoly, Vickie. It's going to be very, very lucrative for us all."

She felt his hands begin to work at the rest of the buttons on her dress. When it slipped to the floor, he stepped back to admire her. "My God," he said, "you're beautiful! A goddess in the flesh."

He unbuttoned his pants and kicked off his boots. Jessie

saw that he was large and erect. She pulled him to her, not giving a damn right now that he probably was going to be her enemy. "How many of us are there in this?" she panted. "I mean . . . how much money are we talking about?"

Grayson eased her down on the huge leather sofa and stripped off her pantalettes. He swallowed loudly and tore off his shirt and tie. "Vickie, baby," he breathed hoarsely, "you treat me right and do what I tell you, and you'll be as rich as you already are beautiful. Not only are we going to sew up the passenger business, but we are going to win ourselves a new government mail contract worth eighty thousand dollars a year."

She reached up and grabbed his manhood and squeezed it, then pulled him down to her. Jessie spread her legs, staring up at his muscular body. It was a body so sculptured with layers of hard muscle that she knew he had to be a physical-fitness fanatic. His body was that of a twenty-year-old laborer, except that his thick chest hair was silver. "You look very good for your age, Orin."

He laughed, gripped her thighs, and spread her open even farther. "Vickie, you are about to find out the best part of me."

Grayson drove his shaft deep inside her and Jessie moaned with the hard feel of him. He was big and stiff, and now, as he began to move his hips in a slow ellipsis, he lowered his head and went back to work on her nipples with his mouth.

Jessie reached down and gripped his powerful buttocks and began to work them to her own motion. She closed her eyes and let the pleasure of their lovemaking overcome her completely. It wasn't easy playing a hard, money-grasping girl like Vickie Wilson, a girl who would do anything to make a lot of money. No, it wasn't easy at all. But she was going to do the best that she could.

He had been on her for almost half an hour and his body had lifted her up almost to a climax again and again before he had slowed his thrusting and brought her back down to a pleasure plane that was nothing short of ecstasy. But now he was again beginning to quicken his rhythm and his thrusting was becoming jerky and ragged.

His breath was coming fast in her ear and Jessie felt her own body losing control, and her long, tapered legs lifted to lock over his hips and drive him faster and faster.

"Oh, Vickie," he choked. "Now! Now!"

Jessie didn't have to be told. She felt his body pounding at her own and then felt his huge manhood spewing hot seed deep into her own hungry cavern of desire. They lifted into a frenzied tower of pleasure and then fell back exhausted, bodies jerking spasmodically for delicious seconds after the act was finally consummated.

"I'll never let you want for anything again, Vickie," Grayson whispered. "You're my woman now. Stay with me and I might even make you my wife. And someday we'll go to Washington, D.C., where you will be a United States Senator's wife. And maybe even a United States President's!"

Jessie nodded, not trusting her voice to speak.

If this man was as good at politics as he was in pleasing a woman, maybe he wasn't exaggerating a bit.

Chapter 6

The four men stood outside Ki's hotel room. It was well after midnight and the hallway was empty and dark because they had snuffed the wall lamps. Their leader struck a match and peered at the room number. Satisfied, he blew out the match and whispered, "Remember, the boss said this time it's just a warning. We don't want to kill the slant-eyed bastard. If he don't learn from the lesson we give him tonight, then we'll finish him off next time."

They grunted their understanding. One of them, a coarse-featured man with a face scarred by the pox, bounced lightly on his feet with anticipation. Satisfied, the leader produced a passkey and carefully inserted it into the door's lock. He felt the lock move and knew it was opening. He did not like Chinamen. Ten years earlier he had been part of a gang of men who had tarred and feathered a bunch of the yellow heathens and driven them out of Reno. Sent them packing into the mountains, howling like the dogs of hell. The leader remembered how much fun that had been and hoped this would be just as unforgettable.

Ki heard the lock turn. He had heard their whispers, too. Only now did he finally select the *nunchaku* sticks. The sticks were a favored samurai weapon. The ones he preferred were shorter than those most commonly used in Japan and were called *han-kei*, which roughly translated in English to mean "half-sized version." The two sticks were halves that fit together neatly and were connected at one end by a few inches of braided horsehair. Instead of them reaching from his palm to his elbow, the *han-kei* were only seven inches long, but incredibly fast in the hands of a martial-arts master. They were easy to conceal and so effectively could Ki make use of them that he could perform every *te* block and strike with the extra power brought to the techniques by the hard wooden *nunchaku* handles. When Ki held one of the handles and whipped the other around in a circular motion it became so dangerous a weapon that the centrifugal force it exerted could crush a skull. In close fighting, the two handles could also be used to break a man's fingers as easily as a walnut caught between the jaws of a nutcracker. But even more than all those things, the *nunchaku* were awesome when used to parry an opponent's blow before stabbing for the soft places of his throat and face.

Ki would also have liked to have used a *bo*, or wooden fighting staff, in this close fighting, for he was considered one of the best to ever master that weapon. But he would not have been able to bring one on the train without having to answer some questions. So the *nunchaku* would be his choice tonight.

The door pushed open and Ki moved behind it so that the men who entered his room passed by him. When they were all inside, he silently closed the door so that the four men were trapped.

"Hey!" one yelled. "The door just closed! He's—"

The man never finished his warning. The rest of the sentence rattled incoherently in his throat as the tips of the *nunchaku* handles found his larynx. He choked. His eyes bulged as he grasped for air that would not immediately come. A horrible sound emanated from him as he fought wildly to breathe. Ki dropped him with a sweeping kick to the knees.

The leader shouted and jumped back as he heard the ominous whirring sound of the hard wooden blades. He clawed for his gun. Suddenly he saw a fire exploding in the darkness and then he was falling with blood cascading down his face from a lacerated and broken nose.

The other two men were faster with their sixguns. Both of them cleared leather and fired, but Ki was suddenly gone. Angry bullets chewed the walls of Ki's expensive hotel room and ripped the beautiful wallpaper apart. A porcelain statue of a horse shattered and smoke lay heavy in the air.

Ki waited until the guns were empty and then he touched a match to the wick of a kerosene lamp that rested on his bedside table. The room filled with flickering light and when the two gunmen saw the slender samurai standing beside the door, they blinked with amazement.

The leader, his ruined face cradled in the palms of his bloodied hands, screamed, "Kill the Chinese bastard. Get him!"

The two gunmen glanced over at the first man, who still lay twitching and clutching his battered throat. Only now was he finally able to get some air to his tortured lungs. Because of the gunsmoke, his terrorstruck face seemed an even more bluish color than it actually was. The two men retreated toward the window and tried to reload their guns.

Ki did not give them the opportunity. He moved swiftly and then he brought his foot up in a sweep-lotus kick. It connected with so much force that one of the men was sent crashing through the window. His high-pitched scream ended suddenly when he hit the street below.

The last man dropped his gun and raised his hands in fear. "Don't kill me, please! I want no more of this. I just want outa here, Mr. Ling!"

Ki, fingers still, body tensed to strike with the speed and the devastation of a diamondback rattler, suddenly relaxed.

"Who hired you?" he asked.

The man opened his mouth, then clamped it shut. Ki stepped forward and the man backed to the wall and held his hands up to protect his face.

"I asked you a question," Ki said. "Who hired you?"

"I did!" the leader screamed, grabbing his gun and cocking it to fire.

Ki swung around and saw that there was not time to reach the man before he pulled the trigger. Ki threw himself sideways and over the bed. The bullet that should have had his name on it ate into the dresser and a second bullet exploded into the kerosene lantern. A shower of fuel and fire covered the bedspread.

"Come on. The place is on fire!" the leader bellowed.

Ki jumped for the small pitcher of water on his washstand. He used the contents on the flames, but it was not enough. He grabbed the bedspread and the flames bit into the flesh of his hand. He balled the bedspread up and raced to the window, where he hurled the flaming mass outside.

It hit the street and men shouted in surprise, then anger as horses tied along the nearest hitching rail bolted in panic and broke their reins to stampede wildly down the street. Ki saw another small knot of men look up at him in shock.

They were congregated around the body of the man who had catapulted through Ki's window only moments earlier. Ki twisted around to see that some of the fire had dropped from the bedspread to the rug, which it was now eating greedily. He looked for something to smother the fire with before it roared out of control. There was no time to go after the three surviving gunmen he could now hear crashing down the stairs into the lobby.

Hotel fires were killers. Ki knew that, for the next few minutes, the only option he had was to stomp out this fire before it spread to other hotel rooms and killed innocent people.

When he finally stamped out the last ember, the room was scorched and smoke-filled. Ki packed up his bags and was just about to leave when the sheriff stepped into the doorway. "What the hell is going on up here!" he demanded, staring at the carnage.

Ki smiled disarmingly. "A little misunderstanding,

Sheriff, that is all. So sorry to have bothered you."

The man stalked into the room and marched over to the shattered window. He stared down into the street to see the dead man. "Yeah," he growled. "That poor bastard came through the window. You want to tell me about it now, or after I book you in jail on the suspicion of murder?"

Ki acted shocked. "I murdered no one. I was attacked by intruders who came bursting into this room without warning."

"Why?"

Ki shrugged. "Money, I suppose."

The lawman glanced at the expensive leather bags and then a little closer at the suit that Ki had just pulled on. Anyone could see that it was custom-tailored and of the finest materials. "Who the deuce are you?"

Ki handed the man a card he had had the foresight to have printed during the Sacramento delay. It identified him as Chen Ling, son of Sam Ling, owner and manager of the Hong Kong Shipping Company.

The sheriff studied the richly embossed card for a long moment. "This is a hell of a long way from the Pacific Ocean, Ling. What the devil are you doing in Reno?"

"I'm here on business." Ki glanced over the sheriff's shoulder to see a crowd of gawkers in the hallway. He would have bet his ceremonial *katana* sword that one of them was an employee of the Sierra Stage Line trying to fathom what could possibly have gone wrong.

"I'm listening. What kind of business?"

Ki shifted as if he were nervous. "Actually, I am here on behalf of my honorable father. He is interested in investing in a stage line."

"A stage line? A Chinaman owning a stage line is crazy! What would your father want to do a fool thing like that for?"

"For the money. Chinese investment money is good in Reno, is it not?"

"Well, sure, but—"

73

"I am here on the invitation of the honorable Mr. Daniel Bonaday. It is his line that my father is interested in as a possible investment."

The sheriff shook his head. "Don't make sense to me. Even less sense is how come you are alive and that poor fella down there is dead."

Ki smiled innocently. "He rushed at me and I jumped aside at the very last minute. He could not stop his momentum and went through the window. It was very sad." Ki sympathetically clucked his tongue against the roof of his mouth.

"It sure as hell was—for him, but not for you. What about the fire? Did he start that, too?"

"As a matter of fact, yes."

The sheriff scowled. He twisted around and glared at the gawkers assembled in the hallway. "I don't suppose any of you folks happened to see what really happened in here?"

They all said that they had not, but one of the guests swore, "There were three or four of them, by God! I heard them raising hell in here and then they all went running down this hall. They hit the stairs like a buffalo stampede and lit out like the devil himself was on their tail!"

The sheriff pinned the hotel's night clerk, who had been on duty in the lobby. "Well," he barked, "is that the truth, or not?"

The clerk gulped nervously. "Yeah," he finally croaked, "there were some men that came up and down in a hurry. But I was reading the newspaper and didn't hardly even get a look at them."

"I yelled, 'Fire!'" Ki said. "I think it quite natural that people on this floor would attempt to leave as fast as they possibly could."

The sheriff hooked his thumbs in his cartridge belt and glared at Ki. The lawman was of average height, in his mid-thirties, and wiry. He had a mustache and long sideburns and his hat was pushed back to reveal black hair heavily pomaded and smelling like freshly crushed green

74

apples. His jaw was square and aggressive, but he looked Ki right in the eye, and the samurai judged the sheriff to be an honest, dependable man. Not clever or particularly perceptive, but a solid man who brooked no nonsense.

He handed back the business card and said, "Mr. Ling, I'm afraid I am going to have to take you to jail and hold you for the night. In the morning, I'll get ahold of Dan Bonaday. If your story checks out, then I'll let you out on your own word that you'll stay around until after I have completed my investigation. That fair enough?"

Ki nodded. "I can't stay here in this room tonight. Of course, Sheriff. My honorable father has always taught me to believe in the justice of this country's laws. Do you intend to handcuff me?"

The sheriff gauged Ki's size and weight and said, "Naw, you try anything, I'll just have to put a hammerlock on you and drag you into the cell. You Chinamen don't like to have your dignity ruffled that way, do you?"

"Only my mother was Japanese. My father was—"

"Don't say it," the sheriff warned abruptly. "Folks don't like to hear about races mixin', especially when it comes to the opium-smokin' Orientals."

Ki turned away to hide his anger because the Japanese did not smoke opium like the Chinese. He had wanted to tell this man that the Japanese and the Chinese were like night and day, like oil and water. That they hated each other and always would. But Ki bit back his words because it would not matter to this man or to any of the others now listening. The only one who would take notice of it would be the spy from the Sierra Stage Line, who would immediately report this perplexing bit of inconsistent information to Orin Grayson, Lee Ford, and anyone else at the top of their dung heap.

The sheriff waited till Ki grabbed his bags. "Step aside," he yelled. "We're coming through. Show is over, you can all go back to bed now."

"What about the damage to this room?" the night clerk wailed. "The rugs are ruined, the window will have to be replaced, and that bedspread down in the street was worth—"

Ki reached into his trousers pocket and found a neatly folded hundred-dollar bill. "I think this ought to be enough to cover the damage," he said with a slight bow of apology. "So sorry to be of such trouble."

The man stared at the money. It was more than he would earn in three months, and many times the amount required to make restitution for the hotel damages. He would pocket the profit and use the rest to buy some new clothes. But none of his great delight showed on his face as he stared at Ki with snobbish disapproval. "You have caused this establishment some embarrassment, Mr. Ling. But we will forgive the transgression and this will, I think, cover the costs."

"George, it had goddamn well better," the sheriff said. "I'll put it in my report and make sure the owner knows how much the Chinaman gave you."

George colored and snapped peevishly, "I'll remember you too, Sheriff! The very next time you need a room and a secret kept, I'll remember real well."

Someone tittered. But the other people in the hall chose to ignore the damning remark and Ki felt himself being shoved down the hallway none too gently.

Jessie had known she would be too late to be of any help to Ki. She had not been able to shake free of Orin Grayson until two in the morning. The man had been an insatiable lover and possessed a remarkable amount of stamina. Furthermore, to have revealed her urgent desire to leave would have raised suspicions. Jessie had gently tried again to seek the names of Grayson's colleagues. All she learned was that they were a group of financiers from Sacramento. That, and the secret that a fat mail contract as well as the possibility of an even more lucrative government contract to haul coinage to and from the U.S. Mint in Carson City were being considered. No wonder the Sierra Stage Line wanted to be a monopoly! Not only would it be able to charge exorbitant prices for passenger and freight travel, but the government contracts guaranteed a high and continuing rate of profit.

Jessie watched Ki being led away past the crowd of onlookers who had come to stare at the body lying broken in the street. She felt a deep flood of relief that almost overrode her guilt for not discovering from Grayson the other investors backing the Sierra Stage Line. At least she now knew what the stakes were and that Bonaday could win this battle and have every expectation of reaping a fair, perhaps even significant profit. The ironic thing to Jessie was that Grayson and Ford had not considered that there was going to be enough business and profit for both stage lines without having to turn to sabotage.

It was greed that drove men to destroy their competitors; greed and ego that drove them to be satisfied with nothing less than total victory over their opponents. Jessie had seen a little bit of the former and a lot of the latter in Alex Starbuck. She had never quite understood it, but she had accepted it as part of the man she loved and admired.

"I asked my pa about you," a voice said close behind her.

Jessie turned on her heel and saw Billy Bonaday standing on the walk with a drink in his big fist. A streetlamp cast a sickly yellowish light that made his face seem sharper than it actually was with his prominent cheekbones and jawline. Jessie saw that he was weaving just slightly and guessed that he had drunk too much this evening.

"What did your father say?" Jessie asked, knowing that it must have been hard for Dan Bonaday to lie to his children but also that they had agreed there was no choice. Looking at Billy now, wild, half drunk, and angry for some reason, Jessie was glad that they had not trusted the Bonaday children. Those two did not seem capable of keeping even the smallest secret.

"He said you were my goddamn cousin, all right. Told me about your mother and how you was illegitimate and everything."

"Does it make any difference now? You know I'm after money and you threw me out of your father's office. I don't see that we have anything to talk about."

Jessie did not want to argue with this man, and so she turned back toward her hotel. In the morning, she could get a message to Ki and—

"Wait a minute, damn it!" Billy snapped, pulling her roughly about. "I want to talk to you, Cousin Vickie!"

She yanked her arm free and slapped him across the face, hard. He rocked back on his heels and Jessie reached inside her purse, ready to pull out her gun. She had never allowed any man to handle her unkindly and she would not start now.

But he did not try to strike back as she expected. Instead, he wiped a trickle of blood from his lip and took a deep breath. He emptied his drink into the dirt and, when it was all gone, pitched the glass into the alley. "I owe you an apology," he said. "So I'm apologizing."

She was still angry. "For what? Tossing me out like a filthy beggar, or bruising my arm just now!"

"For both, and for..." He struggled to find the words. "Well, for what my father did, or I guess didn't do for your mother when she got pregnant. I couldn't believe he'd turn his back on his own blood. On anyone that was down and out like your mother must have been. My pa, well, we fight and I know I don't help him much, but I've always loved and respected the man. Until I learned about this."

The anger washed right out of Jessie. She searched for some way to ease the pain he was obviously in. "Listen, Billy—"

"Bill," he corrected, "whores and old ladies still call me Billy. Men and ladies ought to call me Bill. I'm a man full grown some years now. I may not act like one more'n one day outa every three or four, but I am."

"Why don't you be a little easier on your father," Jessie said. "It happened a long time ago."

"If I had money, I'd give it to you. But I don't. Thought that Mr. Chen Ling was our savior, but now it don't look too good. If he goes to a trial, they'll hang him for no other reason than he's half Oriental."

Jessie blinked. "How could they put him on trial?"

"For tossing that man out his second-story window." Billy's face grew hard. "This is just what Grayson and Ford would have wished for on a goddamn falling star. It's the perfect excuse to get rid of Chen Ling. They'll bribe a judge and then a jury. Ling will be fortunate to escape the gallows before this is all said and done. He's as good as hung now."

Jessie's heart almost stopped. My God! She had not even thought that something like that might happen to Ki. But of course Grayson and Ford would quickly realize the opportunity they had been presented with and capitalize on it at once.

"He'll need the best lawyer in Reno," Jessie said quickly. "Who is he?"

"Name is Don Blake, but he's taken. The man is on a retainer for the Sierra Stage Line Company."

"Then we'll have to find an even better man. One from Sacramento or even San Francisco."

Bill's face brightened. "Sure! Chen Ling's father will gladly pay all the legal expenses." Feeling impulsive and filled with new hope, he reached for Jessie's arm, then pulled his hand away as if he had touched fire. "Didn't mean to touch you, Vickie," he said quickly. "Don't slap me again. Last time, you almost knocked my teeth out."

Despite all the circumstances, Jessie laughed. She really was surprised to see that, underneath that bravado and arrogance, this man had a warm sense of humor and some real human compassion for someone less fortunate than himself.

"I won't hit you. Not unless you try to grab me hard again."

"Not a chance. Will you help me find a lawyer for Chen Ling?"

"Well—" Jessie clamped her mouth shut. My God, she thought, what am I doing! I am working for the Sierra

Stage Line and trying to infiltrate their accounting department to discover all of our enemies. She wanted to crawl away in shame. "I can't, Bill."

The broad smile on his face died. "Well . . . well, why not? I said I was sorry. And if you'll find it in your heart to forgive and forget, I swear we'll help you any way we can. I'll even talk to Pa in the morning and maybe—"

Jessie couldn't bear to hear another word. "Bill," she told him, "after you kicked me out I was so mad I went and got a job with your competition."

He was stunned. He reeled back on his heels and stared at her for a moment in full disbelief. When he realized that she was telling him the truth, a look of utter contempt distorted his handsome features. "Well damn your soul, anyhow! Between you and my sister, Pa and me have had about all the Judas betrayers we can stand."

"Bill, I—"

"Get out of here!" he shouted in a voice so hate-filled and loud that it caused heads to turn. "Go . . . go screw the mighty Mr. Grayson, if you can pry my sister out from under him!"

Jessie felt the heat rise up in her cheeks. His words cut her to the quick and she wanted to grab this man by the neck and tell him the enormous risks that she, Ki, and Bill's father were taking to end the killing, robberies, and sabotage that threatened to break Bonaday's dying stage line.

But she did not. Instead, she turned and ran toward her hotel, because she was not used to men seeing her cry in pain and anger. She would turn her attention to saving Ki. She would make Orin Grayson drop all charges against him and let him go. Orin was under her power now—or if not, he soon would be.

The only joker in the deck that Jessie could see was Roxy Bonaday. Roxy, who was jealous and possessive and fool enough to be used by her own father's enemy. Jessie would have to face Roxy and figure out a way to get her out of the picture.

She slowed at her hotel and walked through the lobby with her head up and her stride long and purposeful. She walked like a Starbuck woman. And tomorrow, she would need to think and act like one as well. Alex Starbuck had drilled self-control into her for years. No tears, no more weakness and feeling sorry for someone like Billy Bonaday.

Jessie entered her room and locked the door. She pressed herself against the door and angrily scrubbed the tears from her eyes with her sleeve. Vickie Wilson was supposed to be a real tough little chippy. All right, but she wasn't half the woman that Jessie was. Jessie, who would portray her in this hell-busted Nevada town right to the bitter end.

Chapter 7

Ki paced restlessly behind the bars of his cell until the door of Sheriff Frank Colton's office burst open before the angry onslaught of Daniel Bonaday. "Goddamnit, Frank, let Chen Ling the hell outa that cell! Why didn't you send someone out to my place last night and tell me there was trouble?"

Sheriff Colton had been about to go out hunting for Bonaday if the man had not arrived within the next few minutes. "Now, simmer down a bit, Dan. I heard Chen's story and I'm ready to accept the fact that it was purely a case of self-defense and of attempted robbery. Chen swears that he had never laid eyes on the man that did a nosedive outa his window into the street. I'm prepared to believe him and let him free. But he has to give me his word that he'll stay here in town until all the questions have been settled to everyone's satisfaction."

A well-dressed man in a black suit, white shirt, and derby hat barged into the open doorway. "And I," he proclaimed dramatically, "am prepared to file first-degree murder charges against that deadly Chinaman!"

Ki blinked and then shook his head. He had been afraid that something like this might happen. During the long night behind bars, he had had plenty of time to think. He was in a fix and Bonaday's enemies weren't the kind to miss an opportunity.

Dan Bonaday's reaction to the Sierra Stage Line attorney was swift and predictable. "Mr. Blake, I'll be damned if I'll let you get away with that ridiculous charge!"

"Bonaday is right," Sheriff Colton said. "Before you can make a charge like that stick, you have to have some proof. Otherwise—"

The attorney poked a smoking cigar at the sheriff and said, "Don't tell me what I need or do not need to make the charge stick, Sheriff. I have a witness who is willing to testify that Mr. Chen Ling and the deceased were well acquainted."

"That's not true!" Ki said angrily. "I never saw the man before. He and three others came to my room to rob me."

"Hold it!" the sheriff bellowed, raising his hands for silence. "Blake, where is this witness of yours?"

"Right here," the attorney said, stepping aside and letting the hotel night clerk step forward.

The sheriff made no attempt to hide both his skepticism and contempt. "George? Last night you told me that you didn't see anything!"

The clerk was little more than a pimply-faced kid, barely out of his teens. Stung by the fact that he was not going to get to pocket the profits from Ki's one hundred dollars, maybe he had decided that he would get even or take a bribe. Either way, Ki knew that George was lying and that he would be well paid to perjure himself in court.

George gulped and continued his lie. "But after I saw the dead man's face, I remembered later how that rich Chinaman and him went upstairs together. They said hello to me when they passed and seemed real friendly."

"That's an outright falsehood," Ki said. "He is lying to you, Sheriff."

"Prove it!" the attorney snapped. "We have a witness who says that the Chinaman and the dead man were acquainted with each other. I suspect they went up to his room and quarreled. Then the Chinaman somehow threw him out of the window. Murder in the first degree."

But the sheriff was not convinced. "There is too much we don't know for a charge like that. No one was in the room who can say what really happened."

"Sheriff Colton, that is not your concern, and I suggest you are way out of line. I'm the attorney-at-law here, and I—"

Dan Bonaday had heard enough. "You money-graspin' sonofabitch! You know you can't get a first-degree murder charge to stick without someone else having been in that hotel room!"

Don Blake was a large man himself and when the two advanced with clenched fists, it took all the sheriff's power to get between them and prevent a fight from breaking out right in his office.

"Stop it!" Colton yelled. "Or so help me, I will jail you both for obstructing the peace!"

He shoved Bonaday and Blake away from each other and glared at George. "Now listen here," he said in a hard voice. "I ain't prepared to believe anything you say, boy. I don't trust you as far as I could—"

"Sheriff Colton!" the attorney bellowed. "I demand that you keep your opinions to yourself and let a judge and jury decide whether or not this witness is telling the truth."

George looked frightened, but he was also resolute. "I'm tellin' the truth, and I'll stand up and swear to it before the court. That man," he said, pointing a shaking finger at Ki, "that man and the dead one were friends. He murdered him."

"How?" The sheriff looked at Ki. "Mr. Chen Ling can not weigh one hundred seventy pounds soaking wet; the man that was tossed out the window was six feet tall and well over two hundred pounds."

The attorney sneered. "The Chinaman is a martial-arts man. I'd bet anything on it. All the rich Chinese have their kids taught in the martial arts to defend themselves. That one may look weak, but I'll bet you he isn't. Isn't that right, Chen?"

Ki said nothing.

"See?" the attorney crowed. "He damn sure knows that he could have used superior quickness and balance to throw a heavier but clumsier opponent through his hotel-room window. But he isn't about to admit that and incriminate himself."

"You aren't going to get away with this," Bonaday growled. "Even if Chen and the dead man did know each other, you can't prove that what happened wasn't self-defense."

"Maybe, maybe not," the attorney said. "But his witness and I are heading over to see Judge Heath right now, and I assure you he will see fit to issue a decision to set a trial date and keep that yellow-skinned killer behind bars!"

The attorney and George left and when the sheriff had closed the door on them, he turned to face Bonaday and Ki. "I have no choice but to wait and see if they are successful in getting the murder charges filed. If Judge Heath signs the order, I'm afraid that you are going on trial for murder, Mr. Ling."

"But damnit!" Bonaday roared. "Judge Heath eats out of Orin Grayson's back pocket. Of course old Heath will issue the order! And Ki . . . I mean, Chen Ling, will be sent to court and then prison as sure as hell is hot!"

Ki did not miss the fact that Bonaday, in his extreme anger, had used his real name. Fortunately, the sheriff did not seem to pick up on that. But what did it matter, anyway? If he was going to be stuck in this jail, he was of no value to anyone. Not to Bonaday and his stage line, and especially not to Jessie. Ki swallowed his bitterness. He tried to think of some way out of this mess, but there was none. And he could not even have prevented this from occurring, because he had been fighting for his life. Sure, he wished now he had not used the sweep-lotus kick that had sent the assassin plunging in a hail of glass to his death. But there had been four of them with guns, and there had not been time to act with anything less than lethal force.

"Sheriff? Can I talk to Mr. Bonaday privately?"

"Sure," Colton sighed. "I'll be outside getting some fresh air. Take your time, Dan. But if you try and slip him a weapon or even a hacksaw blade, then I'll find it and jail you for a month. By then, what you have left of a business will be gone. Think about that before you do anything foolish."

Bonaday flushed but kept his mouth shut until after the door closed. Then he walked over to Ki and gripped the bars. "Hell of a mess you got us into now, Ki."

"*I* got us into?" Ki could not believe his ears.

"Well, sure! What good are you to me behind bars? Now I gotta find a way to get you out of trouble."

Ki bit back his anger. "Get a message to Jessie Starbuck. Tell her that this cell isn't so bad and that the only thing she can do is to push this Judge Heath to set a quick trial date. They can't convict me of anything. Also, there is the matter of the men George said came rushing down from the upstairs hallway. George can't deny he said that, and his statement backs up my own story."

Bonaday shook his head. "You don't seem to understand how the deck is stacked against you, Ki. This is Reno, Nevada, not San Francisco or Texas. Orin Grayson and the judge are very important and powerful men. They can get you convicted and sent to prison. They can and they will."

Ki shook his head. "Jessie won't ever let that happen. She'll hire a dozen of the finest lawyers anywhere if that's what it takes to overturn the conviction."

"You may be right. But it'll drag out in one courtroom after the other and by then, by God, I will be dead of old age and you will have gray hair instead of black. Don't you see? Even if you eventually win, we've lost." Bonaday slipped a derringer out of his boot top. "Take this and—"

"Uh-uh. I don't need a gun," Ki told the man. "I can escape whenever I want."

"How?" Bonaday asked with a suspicious look. "Sheriff Colton ain't brilliant, I'll grant that, but he's not stupid either."

"I know. But you heard him. He doesn't believe for one minute that I am strong enough to have thrown a man to his death. He underestimates me. That is the key."

"Yeah, well, let me tell you this, Ki. After last night, Colton might underestimate you, but you can bet that he is the only one!"

Ki agreed with reluctance. After overcoming the four men they had sent to his room last night, Grayson, Ford, and whoever else he was up against would not ever make the same mistake of underestimating his fighting ability. But for right now, none of that really mattered. He was in jail until the trial was over. Then, win or lose, Jessie would see that he was free again.

At the moment the telegraph office had opened that morning, Jessie had sent an urgent message to her old friend and bank president, Mr. Friendel, care of the Bank of San Francisco. The message had been very brief, but there was enough to let the banker know that he was to engage and send the finest legal mind to Reno, Nevada, immediately. The lawyer was to be paid and employed by Daniel Bonaday.

Afterward, Jessie had gone to work in the Sierra Stage Line office under the direction of Peter Bakemore, who was nearly giggly with happiness. Jessie spent the entire first two days listening to the accountant explain his complex system of record-keeping. She had easily followed the explanations and even had to admit that Bakemore was a brilliant accountant, one far underpaid and unappreciated. He had set up a system of double bookkeeping that was in perfect order and then created several ingenious peripheral systems of additional checks and balances. Figures were not the things that Jessie enjoyed most in life, but she did know enough to realize the man was an accounting wizard. When this was all over, if it were determined that Peter Bakemore was completely innocent of any wrongdoing, then she knew that she wanted this man on her own payroll.

True to all predictions, Judge Heath had written the order to the sheriff that ordered Ki retained in jail for trial. A date had been set for two months in the future, but Jessie was confident that the San Francisco attorney she had sent for would get the trial date moved up considerably. His name was Lawrence Applegate and Jessie had seen him on the street with Dan Bonaday soon after his arrival in Reno. Physically, at least, the California attorney was not impressive. Of average height, build, and looks, he was in his early forties, with sand-colored hair and blue eyes. He dressed nicely, but was not a fashion plate like many of San Francisco's legal lions. He carried a black, accordion-type briefcase that bulged with papers and legal tomes. He looked intelligent and intense, and Jessie did not doubt for a minute that he was the best.

The trouble was, she could not dare to pay the man a visit. In fact, she had let Bonaday know that Applegate was not to be made privy to the fact that it was the famous Jessica Starbuck who was his real employer.

News came at the end of the week that the trial date had been moved up. Jessie was in the Sierra Stage Line office when Orin Grayson shouted, "Damn Judge Heath! Why did he do a stupid thing like that!"

"Because that new attorney of Bonaday's found some law on the books that said there was not enough evidence to support a trial for murder. He swore he would move to have the judge removed from his bench if he did not try the case next week."

"And the judge believed him?"

"He had to. Apparently, Applegate showed the judge the legal precedent and made it clear he had friends, both here and in California, who would see to it that he either agreed to the earlier trial date, or he would be made to look like an ignorant fool."

"Damn!" Grayson shouted. "Heath is getting senile. When this is over, I'm going to see that he retires so that we can get someone smarter and with considerably more backbone on the judge's bench."

Grayson stepped out into the main office. "Miss Wilson, I want to speak to you at once."

Jessie smiled at Bakemore, who was right in the middle of another explanation. She almost welcomed the excuse to leave, but she was nervous whenever Grayson wanted to see her. Since that first night together when she had tried to get him to divulge who else was behind the conspiracy against the Bonaday Stage Line, they had spoken only briefly. Roxy Bonaday had taken one look at Jessie and had hovered around Grayson continually ever since.

Now, as Jessie walked in to see Grayson, the assemblyman was clearly agitated. "Vickie," he said, closing the door behind her and motioning her to a seat, "please sit down and let's talk. First, I'm sorry that I have been ignoring you. Believe me, you've been on my mind night and day."

"You've been very well occupied," Jessie said, making it sound as if she were jealous.

"You mean by Miss Bonaday?"

"Yes. She is lovely."

"Sure, but after having you, I see the difference between a girl and a woman. When this is over and I have bankrupted and driven the entire Bonaday family out of Nevada, we can make up for lost time. Right now, though, I don't want anything to make Roxy more jealous than she already is. Do you know what the girl wants me to do?"

"No."

Grayson sighed. "She wants me to have our attorney, Mr. Blake, drop the murder charges against Chen Ling. Can you imagine that!"

"But why?"

"The girl is all mixed up. She wants to marry me and . . . well, of course, I am sort of leading her on in order to keep her loyalty. I've told her that I have offered to buy her father out, and that right before he is due to lose everything, I'll bail him out financially."

"And she believed you?" Jessie was astounded at Roxy's gullibility.

"Yeah. I even set up a bank account with both our names on it. The account is to go to her father the day he agrees to quit his business. Also, I have promised to see that the Bonaday stagecoaches and all their physical assets are not impounded by the courts for the satisfaction of bad debts. You see, Dan Bonaday is a pretty sick man. Bad heart. He's had several attacks and Roxy is the only one who knows about them. She thinks that her father is killing himself and ought to get out of business at any price. I, of course, fully agree."

Jessie sat still, letting the impact of what she had just learned sink in fully. This explained so very, very much. Now she understood Roxy Bonaday a little and found herself feeling sorry for the foolish girl rather than just despising her for betraying her own father. Roxy was in love with Grayson—for that, she could not be faulted. Despite their age differences, Grayson was debonaire, handsome, and absolutely peerless as a lover. A girl like Roxy, who might have been a virgin when she fell into the assemblyman's clutches, would soon become helpless to resist his charms and persuasive powers.

"Are you sure about the bad heart?"

"Of course! Roxy says that the only ones who know about it are the family doctor and us—you're the fourth one, and I don't want you to say a word. Old Dan is too proud to even tell his son, Billy."

"What do you want me to do?"

"I want you to go see Bonaday. Tell him that you regret what has happened and realize what a fool you were to come to work for me. Ask him to give you a job."

"He won't do it. And even if he did, Billy hates me now."

"Change his opinion." Grayson leaned forward. "This is between the two of us. Don Blake says we haven't got a chance of convicting Chen Ling for murder. The best we can do is to get him a short jail sentence. And quite frankly, that might backfire. We could even make him angry enough to stay right here in Nevada and pour money

91

into the Bonaday lines. I can't afford to let that happen."

"But—"

"Let me finish, Vickie. Once you get back in their good graces, find out everything about the Chinaman that you can and report it back to me. Maybe we can buy him off or strike a deal—he agrees to leave Nevada for good, we agree to drop the charges."

"And if he won't agree?"

Grayson shrugged. "We underestimated him once, but we won't a second time. The man is dangerous. We want him out of the picture."

"Who is 'we'?" Jessie dared to ask boldly.

Grayson's eyes drew down to slits. "My dear, lovely money-grasping young lady, there is one thing you have to remember. It is definitely not smart to ask questions that don't need to be asked. You must never want to know more than is necessary. It just puts you under a greater risk. Do you understand what I am saying?"

Jessie nodded. She understood. Understood, too, that she was going to come back into this office tonight and go through the files that she had not seen yet.

"Come here a second," Grayson said with a wink that left little doubt he wanted to kiss her—or worse. The office had a window, but it was high enough that he could explore her privately from the waist down without being observed from the outer office.

Jessie laughed and shook her head. She gestured out the window. "I can't. Bakemore is a very suspicious man and a little possessive. He'd guess what you were doing to me and it would cause all sorts of havoc."

"The man is a frustrated little . . . you ever see his wife?"

"No."

"She's a real hard woman and one that probably puts an apron on him the moment he walks in his front door. She wears the pants in that family, and during the daytime she earns a little money on the side by having men visit her through the back door. No wonder a beautiful, soft-spoken

92

woman like you is driving him half crazy."

Jessie shrugged as if that were of no concern to her as she turned and walked out the door. Her mind was already on the sudden turn of events brought about by Grayson's request that she spy for the Sierra Stage Line. She felt real hope for the first time in a week. With any luck, there would be no trial and Ki would be free very soon. Just yesterday there had been another holdup on the run between Carson City and Genoa that had netted the highwaymen five thousand dollars in gold. Ki would be wanting to ride the coaches and put a stop to that sort of thing. And maybe, Jessie thought, after I go to work for the Bonaday Stage Line, I can help, too.

Chapter 8

Roxy Bonaday had inherited her father's no-nonsense way of approaching problems. She had been watching Jessie and Orin Grayson through the office window and had not been pleased. Even a blind person could have seen that Orin was attracted to Vickie Wilson.

Jealousy was an emotion Roxy had only experienced once, and that was in the seventh grade over a boy named Benny Overman. Roxy had grown up full-bodied and high-spirited. Her hair was dark brown, her eyes large and almond-shaped. She would have been considered beautiful had it not been for the almost masculine strength of her jawline and the fact that her nose was a little larger than was fashionable. Roxy was not the kind of girl a mild fellow would be attracted to. She laughed a little too loudly, enjoyed off-color jokes, and liked big and aggressive men. She also felt strongly attracted by a man who had the guts to take what he wanted—Orin Grayson was exactly that kind of man. The fact that he was much older than she was did not matter a whit.

Roxy had dated and even slept with men her own age, and found them selfish in bed—much too quick to satisfy their own hunger and too slow to help her do the same. Orin was the first man who had shown her how patience could unlock the doors of pleasure for a woman. Before

Roxy had met and gone to bed with Orin, she had believed that sex was totally a giving act for a woman, another obligation that the weaker sex reluctantly gave to the stronger. Roxy loved Orin for teaching her differently, and also because he was going to save her father from being ruined by the Sierra Stage Line.

There were many days when Roxy felt as if she were a martyr. Both her father and her brother had almost disowned her for her involvement with Grayson. They would never have believed that Orin loved her, and that his love would be the salvation of the Bonaday family. Dan and Billy were too proud to accept help from Orin, but they'd need it after the Bonaday Stage Line was auctioned off to pay the creditors.

But what if Vickie Wilson, if that was really her name, captured Orin's love and loyalty? Then, everything Roxy had worked for, all the misguided hurt she had endured from her father and brother would be for nothing. She might even end up as broke and bitter as her father and Billy.

The idea of a stranger like Vickie Wilson destroying everything for her family was too much for Roxy to accept. And so when Jessie left the office to go to lunch, Roxy followed her outside and down the boardwalk.

"Hey!" she called, running to catch up with her. "I want to talk to you!"

Jessie turned to see the girl. Roxy was not more than five or six years younger than herself, but to Jessie, the Bonaday girl seemed like a child. Learning that Roxy was mistakenly trying to help her father helped, but it did not change the impression Jessie had of a foolish, rather spoiled girl.

"I don't want you to be seeing Orin alone anymore," Roxy said, coming right to the point. "I don't believe you are really my cousin, or that your name is Vickie Wilson. And most of all, I don't like you."

They were of the same height, even the same build, although Jessie's waist was a little slimmer and she was a few pounds lighter in the hips. Now, as their eyes locked, Jessie said, "Miss Bonaday, I hope you believe me when I tell you that I have absolutely no designs on Orin Grayson. I assume that is your main concern."

"I'm not jealous," Roxy said defensively. "If Orin wants you more than me, then he can have you with my blessings."

"Don't be ridiculous. Orin and Mr. Ford have given me employment. Nothing else. But for your information, I am quitting the Sierra Stage Line as of today."

Roxy's brown eyes widened with surprise. "Why? I thought you were broke and needed the money."

"I do. I just feel guilty about working for your father's competitors. I'm going to ask him once more for a job. If he declines, then I'll find some other way to support myself."

Roxy frowned with puzzlement. Jessie had caught her off-balance and she was still trying to recover. The carefully made-up speech she had rehearsed to tell Jessie off now seemed ridiculous. "Maybe we ought to go eat together and have a nice, private talk," she said.

Jessie smiled. "I think that would be a fine idea." What Jessie would really have liked to do was tell this girl what a fool she was being for trusting Orin Grayson to be fair and merciful once he had destroyed the Bonaday Stage Line. That was the height of wishful thinking. Once the Bonaday line was bankrupt, Grayson, Ford, and the rest of their backers would snap up the coaches, harness, and horses at a fraction of their value and then reap the profits.

Their lunch was private and adequate, and by the time it was over they had made their peace. "I'll go with you to talk to my father," Roxy said. "Maybe I can put in a good word."

"It's not your father I'm concerned about," Jessie said. "It's your brother. I think he hates me."

"I don't believe that for a minute," Roxy said. "And even if it was true, once Billy sees that you have decided to quit working for the Sierra Stage Line, he'll be more than happy to forgive and forget. You should know that my father won't pay you much of a wage. Not unless Mr. Chen Ling is set free and decides to invest in our business."

Roxy shook her head. "But I don't think either of those things will happen. Mr. Ling isn't stupid. He would only have to look at the books to see that my father's business is busted—if there were any books."

"No record-keeping system, huh?"

"Nothing much," Roxy admitted. "All three of us are terrible with figures. Maybe you could help us out that way."

Jessie nodded. "Tell your brother that for me."

"I will," Roxy promised, "but it's my father's business, and what he decides is what counts. I just wish he would have sold out and retired to a rocking chair years ago."

"Maybe he's one of those men who will never slow down." Jessie knew that this girl was thinking about her father's heart condition and trying to do what she thought was right. "Roxy, there are a lot of men who would rather work right up to the moment that they are called to meet their Maker."

"My dad was once a pretty rich man over in San Francisco," Roxy said, unable to conceal her pride. "He had a fleet of sailing ships and then a so-called friend, a man named Alex Starbuck, stabbed him in the back."

Jessie shook her head. She was shocked to hear that Roxy thought Alex had betrayed Dan Bonaday's friendship. Jessie knew with dead certainty that this was not the case. Over in San Francisco, Mr. Friendel would verify that as the truth. Roxy needed to know the truth, but this was not the time or the place for it.

"Vickie, my father has always operated on a handshake. That's all he ever asked for. Well, when Alex Starbuck broke Dad's fleet of ships, we came to Reno. That's when Dad had his first . . ."

Roxy could not finish, so Jessie did it for her. "His first

98

sign of a failing heart condition? Is that what you were going to say?"

Roxy nodded. "But don't tell anybody. Not even Billy knows. I saw Dad fall when it happened the first time. He groaned and grabbed his chest. We were alone and he fell in the snow. All the blood left his face and he began to shake and water ran off his face. He almost died. I made the doctor tell me the truth—it was a heart attack."

"And that's why you want him out of the business?"

"Yes," Roxy said. "No matter what the cost. But don't tell anybody. You see how my father is. He's big and strong, and a man like that—well, he can't stand to have people thinking he's weak in the heart."

Jessie reached out and squeezed her hand. "I understand, and I won't say anything," she promised. "But I do think you should allow your father to try to save his stage line. It's his whole life. You can imagine how he must feel having already lost a shipping company. I think that, for a man like your father, it's more important than anything else in the world to go out a winner. To leave you and Billy something besides a stack of unpaid bills reaching clear up to the ceiling."

"To hell with the bills! I believe I have figured out a way to handle that part of it. And even if I hadn't, it wouldn't matter. We are talking about my father's life. It's time he retired to enjoy what few years he might have left."

Jessie said nothing more. She could understand Roxy's concern, but her trying to be the one to make the decision about how her father spent his last years was wrong. Especially when she was helping his enemy destroy everything he had worked to build in Nevada. Jessie walked on, knowing that she would somehow have to teach Roxy that, although you needed to love your mother and father as long as they were alive, you had no right to control them.

• • •

99

"I don't give a damn, Pa! This woman is just out to take your money. She's got no loyalty!"

Daniel Bonaday slammed his big fist down on the countertop. "Billy!" he shouted. "My mind is made up. I'm giving her the job of taking care of the books and that's the end of this conversation. Hell, even your own sister has decided we ought to give Vickie a chance."

"Well, that sure as hell ain't no character recommendation. Roxy is sleeping with Orin Grayson, too!"

Roxy lunged at her brother and raked his cheek with her nails. When Billy jumped back, throwing his hands up to protect his eyes, Roxy kicked him in the shins. Bonaday had to separate his two children to keep them from swinging at each other.

"Get the hell out of here, Roxy!" the old man choked, trying to hold his son back.

Suddenly, Bonaday stiffened. His eyes bulged, and then he collapsed. One minute he had been towering between his two offspring, the next he was lying on the floor gasping for breath and as pale as a marble tombstone.

"Get the doctor!" Roxy cried. "Get him quick!"

Billy took off like a streak while Jessie knelt beside the old stage-line owner and took his pulse. It was weak and fluttering like the wings of a butterfly. Roxy began to cry. Jessie prayed silently until the doctor arrived.

"Is he still alive?" the doctor asked, bursting through the door with Billy right behind him.

"Just barely," Jessie whispered as the man pulled out his stethoscope and listened to Bonaday's labored heartbeat.

"Let's get him to bed," the doctor ordered. "Quick!"

Billy picked up his father and carried him into a back room. He laid the big man down on a cot where the doctor covered him up with a woolen blanket. Bonaday looked to be unconscious, barely alive.

"What the hell is wrong!" Billy cried.

"It's his heart," the doctor explained. "This is maybe his third major attack and, by the looks of things, the worst. I don't give him more than twenty-four hours to live."

Billy looked desolated and Roxy worse when she said, "Isn't there anything we can do?"

"You want to call a minister, I'd do it now."

"No," Billy said. "That ain't his way."

The doctor shrugged. "Then perhaps you and Roxy ought to pray for him yourselves. Meanwhile, I got a man on the operating table in a lot of pain. I'll be back as soon as I can."

Roxy grabbed his sleeve and her face was wild. "You can't just leave him now!"

"I have to." The doctor gently pulled his arm away. "I'll be back as soon as possible. If he asks for anything, give it to him. Sometimes whiskey is good for the pain."

When the doctor left, Jessie closed the door behind him and Bonaday opened his eyes. They were clear and bright with intense pain. The man surprised them all when he said, "You heard the doc—I can have whiskey, so bring me that bottle in my desk drawer."

They brought it to him and Roxy held it to his lips while he drank steadily. When he began to choke, Roxy pulled it away and Jessie wiped his lips dry. She had seen men like this before. The whiskey had given Bonaday some of his color back, but it was just a momentary flush. Even as they watched, the deathly pallor returned. Jessie knew the doctor had been overly generous when he said twenty-four hours. Dan Bonaday was failing rapidly and would not last an hour.

As if echoing her thoughts, Bonaday said, "Listen to me closely, children, 'cause this is the last I'm going to say to you. Roxy, I've understood what you were trying to do and that made it tolerable. But now, there is no need to be around that Grayson fella. Once I am gone, he'll come after Billy and what's left of this company like a wolf smelling a wounded buck in deep snow."

"No, he promised me that—"

"Goddamn it, the man's promise means—unhh!"

Bonaday stiffened and his eyes rolled up in his head for a minute. Jessie grabbed the man's thick wrist and felt for a

101

pulse she could not immediately find. But Bonaday came back and when his eyes opened, they all knew it was for the last time. There would be no more foolish protests or arguments.

It was almost five minutes before Bonaday could summon up the will to speak again. "Billy," he whispered.

"Yeah, Pa?"

"You're the president of this stage line now. The boss. You've always had a stubborn streak, wanting to do everything your own way. Now you can. But you got to promise me one thing."

"Name it."

"You'll give Vickie a job and let her do it her own way. You'll trust her, Billy. I don't care what you think, trust her!"

Billy looked up and Jessie could feel his smoldering anger and resentment. But this was a dying man's request, his own father's last request, and so Billy choked, "I promise. And I'll beat them, Pa. I'll use my brains and a gun if I have to, and I will beat them!"

Dan Bonaday nodded and a faint smile touched the corners of his lips. "You two young'uns are in for some big surprises and I wish I could be here when they come. That Chinaman, make him stay too. He's a good man, better even than you think. Use him, Billy. Trust him and Vickie and then fight like hell to win! Roxy, you stay away from our enemies and help your brother!"

Jessie saw how the girl wanted to protest that Orin Grayson was an honorable man. Roxy desperately wanted to tell her father that she had Grayson's sacred vow that the Bonaday Stage Line would be sold for a fair price, but to her credit, Roxy just nodded her head in agreement. "Yes, Father."

"Vickie?"

Jessie leaned forward to hear better. "I loved Alex Starbuck. He was the best man I ever knew and he won fair."

"I know," Jessie said, feeling her own eyes sting.

102

Bonaday had grown weaker with each final word. Now, like a balloon that had gone flat, the man seemed small and deflated. He closed his eyes, choked, "Give the bastards hell!"

And he died.

Chapter 9

They were stalling. Ki should have been released that very afternoon but Judge Heath, in some petty show to demonstrate that he had not capitulated completely, refused to sign the orders.

"Billy, I'm sorry," the sheriff said, "but until I have the order in my hand, I can't let Mr. Ling go free."

The San Francisco attorney was furious, and it showed in his eyes as he said, "Mr. Bonaday, I know how you and your sister are feeling after your father's death. But if you want, I could try to threaten Judge Heath into letting Mr. Ling out today."

Billy thought it over. "I know Heath. He gets his back up far enough, he might just go fishing for a week, and there we'd be."

"That's the chance we take,"

"It's not worth it," Ki said through the bars. "Twelve more hours and I'll have the charges dismissed. It isn't worth risking a week for that short an amount of time. Leave the judge be tonight."

The sheriff nodded. "That'd sure be my recommendation. Like you say, Bill, the judge can get right stubborn. Once he gets it in his mind to resist something, he won't budge."

"Are you sure he told you that he'd definitely be by in

the morning to sign the release papers?" the attorney asked again.

"That's right. And the judge is a man of his word."

Billy moved over to the cell. His father had not been dead four hours and yet he seemed to have aged years. Gone was the jaunty swagger, the cocky boldness that had marked him in the past. Now, he spoke in a no-nonsense way and came straight to the point. "Mr. Ling, we have to talk business right now. With the death of my father, there will be a line of creditors from here to the edge of town. What I have to know is, are you going home to San Francisco on the first train, or are you still interested in investing in the Bonaday Stage Line?"

Ki did not hesitate, because he knew exactly what Jessie's wishes would be. "I'd like to stay and find out more about the business. I cannot speak to my father until I have very carefully studied the business."

"I can have what books there are brought over to you, and you can study them right here in the jail cell and give me an answer. Hell, we don't keep much in the way of records. In ten minutes, you'll know everything. And I won't hold back the debts we owe, either, Mr. Ling. I'll deal honestly with you. Just the same way my father would have."

"I appreciate that. But if the books have not been well kept, they are of little value. What I need to do is to learn something firsthand about the business."

"You'd have to ride the stagecoaches to do that. I lost another couple of drivers as soon as they learned my father died. Most of the employees we had left were just too ashamed to quit because they owed my father favors. I'm afraid that neither Roxy or I are owed that kind of loyalty. There ain't much of a company left at all. I couldn't guarantee you any safety. I can't even afford to hire shotgun guards."

"I would not be afraid to be your, what did you call it?"

Billy forced a smile. "Shotgun guard. But that is impossible. Like I said, it's a damned dangerous job. If anything

106

happened to you, quite honestly, we'd have to close the doors tomorrow. About all we have left is me, Roxy, that damned phony cousin, Vickie Wilson, and—"

Ki frowned. "Miss Wilson is working for you?"

"I had no choice," Billy said, his tone of voice leaving little doubt that he did not want to discuss the matter further.

The attorney looked at Ki. "Mr. Ling, I will, of course, remain here in Reno as long as there is any possibility that I'll be needed."

"Thank you," Ki said. "But I don't think that will be necessary once I am released."

After they left, Ki sat back down on his bunk and stared up at the window. He watched night fall and saw the first star appear in the south. He felt a little depressed because he had been sure he would gain his freedom this night. But he'd been wrong.

Ki wondered why Jessie had left the Sierra Stage Line and gone to work for the Bonadays. How could she find out who was financing the Sierra Stage Line if she could not gain access to their records? Being locked in this cell had been difficult enough without so many questions remaining unanswered. But tomorrow, tomorrow he and Jessie would both be rejoined with the Bonadays. They would each have to play their separate roles, but at least they could watch each other's backs.

With that comforting thought, Ki lay down on his bunk and laced his hands behind his head. He would try to sleep.

"Hey, Mr. Ling?"

Ki sat up. "Yes?"

"I got a sick wife at the house. I'm going to go look in on her for a while. I'll lock the front door so you won't be bothered. If the wife is still real sick I may be pretty late, but don't worry. I'll have your breakfast long before Judge Heath arrives to set you free."

"Thanks. I hope your wife is feeling better."

Sheriff Colton nodded. "I think she will be. Fever was down late this afternoon. Sure too bad about old Dan Bonaday. We lost one of a kind with that man."

Ki nodded and lay down again. He heard the door shut and the sheriff tromp off into the darkness. Ki thought about Jessie and wondered if she was asleep yet. The fact that she owned Dan Bonaday and not his offspring a favor would mean nothing to Jessie. A debt to the former was a debt to the latter. Jessie was a Starbuck, and they were the best sort of friends in this world, or the worst kind of enemies. It would be good to see her again.

Jessie waited until well after dark before she left her hotel room and headed for the offices of the Sierra Stage Line. She had considered waiting until after midnight but had rejected the idea. A woman out alone on the streets that late would invite advances and a considerable amount of interest. No, it was far better to act as if she were going out to meet an escort for a late dinner somewhere. Then, if the Sierra Stage Line offices were closed and darkened, she could enter using the key she had taken. The other obvious advantage of going now was that she would have almost the entire night to search for the names she hoped to find. Orin Grayson had said they were names of prominent men from Sacramento. That helped a great deal. She would need to know their identities, because men who invested heavily in a business were not likely to sit still and let their investments fail. This, Jessie thought, was the primary reason why she had to know who and how many were the men she was dealing with.

With a list of names, she would be able to defend herself or the Bonaday Stage Line against retaliation. When you killed a rattlesnake you didn't just chop off the rattles —you severed the head too, and you buried the damn thing.

She was fortunate enough to engage a surrey that carried her up Virginia Street and over the flowing Truckee River. When she was just a short block away, she ordered the driver to pull over in front of a nice restaurant and paid him a modest tip because she was not supposed to have much money.

"Much obliged. You need a ride back, miss?"

"I'm not sure," she hedged.

The driver was an older man with silver hair and a round, sun-beaten but jovial face. "If there's young bachelors with eyeballs in that eatin' place then I'll wager you won't need my services again tonight, miss!"

Jessie smiled and left. When the driver disappeared around a corner, she changed directions and headed for the Sierra Stage Line offices, praying that they would be dark and deserted. If they were not, she would have to find some respectable establishment to wait in until the stage-line offices were empty.

They were deserted when she reached them and Jessie was thankful. She knew the place well and also knew that there was a hostler who had a dog. The hostler and his watchdog guarded the horses, harness, and wagons out in the back lot. Jessie knew that she might be spotted by the dog if she tried to go around and enter the back door. There being no other choice, she walked straight up to the front door as if she owned the place.

The key slipped in easily and she turned the lock and quickly stepped into total darkness. Jessie was familiar with the lay of the office and had no trouble moving through the outer room and into the smaller office used by Orin Grayson. She would start there and, if she found nothing in the big wooden file cabinets, she would move into Lee Ford's office and search there. The office also had a safe, but Jessie did not believe that what she sought would be locked up. No, unless they thought someone was specifically seeking the names of important Sacramento financiers, they would have no reason to put that kind of information in the safe.

Jessie lit a lamp and turned the wick down very low. She set the lamp on the floor and opened the bottom file. It was bulging with papers. She sighed, hoping that it was not going to be a long evening. Then she began to read.

It took her almost an hour to finish going through Grayson's office, and she learned quite a bit about the man and the company. Grayson, it seemed, had once been worth a considerable amount of money, which had been tied up in land and real estate. He had mortgaged everything and invested heavily in Comstock Lode gold and silver futures. Those futures had proved very costly when the mines had finally begun to play out, and Grayson had nearly been ruined. But he had somehow gotten back on his feet with a series of large loans a few months ago. Unfortunately, the source of those loans was not revealed by the documents she studied.

Jessie moved into Lee Ford's office and found that his file cabinets were locked. She drew a small penknife out of her purse along with a thin wire probe about the length and diameter of an ice pick. Within fifteen seconds she had the bottom file open and started going over the papers. It took her another hour and two files before she found the names of the men she was searching for. There were just three and, as she memorized them, she realized that their presence on a written document was probably an oversight.

Jessie sighed with gratitude. She could telegraph a very good detective agency she had previously used in San Francisco and have men on the way to investigate the three Sacramento financiers at once. Within a few days, a week at the most, she would know if they were just businessmen in the habit of financing highly speculative out-of-state ventures, or if they were actually participants in the dangerous game of sabotage and destruction of the Bonaday Stage Line. She was sitting on the floor debating whether or not to continue through the files in hopes of finding out the exact extent of the outside financing when the sound of a cocking gun froze her blood.

"Miss Wilson! It's you!"

Jessie swung around to see the accountant, Peter Bakemore, standing with a gun wobbling around in his bony fist. He started to lower the weapon, then he raised it back

110

up again. "Miss Wilson, shame on you for stealing from the company files!"

Jessie expelled a deep breath. She was furious at herself for being so absorbed by the files that she had allowed herself to be surprised. But she was also deeply relieved that this was Bakemore and not Grayson or Lee Ford. Especially Ford, whom her looks and charm had no sway over at all. Jessie had a hunch that Lee Ford would have shot her without asking for an explanation that she could not have conjured up anyhow.

She made herself smile gaily. "Well, you caught me, Peter. We accountants just can't stay away from our figures, can we?"

It was a wasted act. "You're not here on business. You have no right to be here at this hour."

Jessie stood up. By the way the gun in Bakemore's fist was shaking, it was clear to her that she was in great danger of being accidentally shot to death. "Yes I do," she said. "I am still working for this company. Mr. Grayson simply thought I would be of more value working for our competition."

"You mean as a spy?"

Jessie nodded.

"I don't believe that. Mr. Grayson and Mr. Ford are very . . . firm, yes, firm and tough businessmen, but they would not spy."

"Why not? They've done everything else but murder the Bonadays. They have sabotaged their coaches, run off their horses, cut their harness, and set up stage robberies so frequently that—"

"That is not true!"

"It is. That's why I am here."

"Who are you really, Miss Wilson? Please don't lie to me anymore. I trusted you. I gave you my sincerest recommendation and now . . . I find you like this. You have betrayed the Sierra Stage Line and me as well!"

Jessie saw the misery on this man's face. She felt sorry for him, but also liked his surprising loyalty to a couple of crooks who treated him shabbily. "Peter, I need your help."

"No! You asked for it once, and what did it earn me but this? I must find and tell my employers at once and let them decide your punishment."

"Peter!" Jessie put some iron into her voice. "If you tell them what I was doing, my life will be in great danger. They will try to kill me."

"That's ridiculous! You haven't gotten anything of value. All our petty cash is in the vault and the real money is in the bank across the street."

"I wasn't after the money." Jessie looked at the gun. "Will you please put that down before it goes off and I am shot? You are a man. If I tried to escape, you could easily stop me."

"I'm not so sure of that, Miss Wilson. You look, well, strong, too."

She allowed herself to smile. "In addition to what?"

"To being . . . beautiful, Miss Wilson. But that won't stop me from doing my duty!" he added quickly.

Jessie sat back down on the floor and turned the wick of the lamp down until there was very little light in the room.

"What are you doing that for?" he asked nervously.

"I don't want any more visitors. I want to talk to you for a few minutes. My real name is Jessica Starbuck. Does that mean anything to you, Peter?"

He blinked. "Of course. Everyone has heard of the Starbuck empire. It is a huge conglomerate, with offices around the world."

"Exactly. And I own it."

"That's preposterous!"

"Is it?" Jessie slipped off a ring she wore. "Look at the design of this closely. At first, it means nothing, but examine it very carefully, then read the inscription engraved underneath the band."

"Turn the light up a little," he said, trying to balance the gun and take the ring at the same time. To Jessie's surprise he succeeded, and after a long time he handed the ring back to her and said, "All right, so it says 'From Alex to

112

Jessica with love.' It could be anyone."

"With a circle star design? One that is known world-wide?"

He swallowed. "Maybe you found it or . . . or yes, damn it, you stole it, just like you were stealing something in here when I arrived. You're a professional thief, that's it!"

Jessie frowned. "What if I am telling the truth about myself? That I really am Jessica Starbuck and the men you work for are violent criminals, men who have used every illegal, immoral, and unethical trick in the book to ruin Dan Bonaday and drive his operation under? What if that is true?"

He stared at her for a long minute. He bit his knuckles nervously and then said, "Then I must resign or risk going to prison!"

"You can help me and I will give you a better job than you ever dreamed of. One at twice the salary. One with your own staff."

His eyes were filled with wonder behind his glasses. "You mean it? You're not just saying that to . . . to get my gun and kill me?"

"I mean it. No charity. You'll earn every penny of your wages. I will send you to be trained in London, then—"

"Oh, my God!" he giggled. "This is like a dream come true. Wait until I tell my wife!"

"No!" Jessie lowered her voice. "You must tell no one until this is all finished. Do you understand me?"

He nodded vigorously.

"Good." Jessie smiled. "Now, help me put away these files and let's call it a night before someone else comes to visit this office."

"But I can't!"

"Why not?"

"I . . . I came here because I'm behind on my work. I have to . . ."

Jessie shook her head. There was no use arguing with the man. But he was going to make her a star employee.

Chapter 10

It was after midnight and Ki was still wide awake. He was thinking about his childhood again, and about his mother and father. Ki barely remembered how his American father had looked. Only that he had been tall and handsome, with a wide smile and strong arms. His mother had been high-born, a member of an aristocratic Japanese family. Ki had no pictures, but the image he retained from long ago was of a woman lovely and gracious. Long, shining black hair, a heart-shaped face with dignity that was the product of centuries of royal Nipponese blood. His mother's single mistake and her great tragedy had been falling in love with the American sailor and marrying him. This had caused her family great anguish, for the Yankee barbarians were considered a vastly inferior race. Disgraced and abandoned by her own people, Ki's mother had not shed a tear because her love for the Yankee consumed her every waking hour. Ki was born during their first year of marriage. Like many Eurasians, Ki was a beautiful child, the product and mix of the best of both races. Yet, for five long years Ki had suffered the mockery heaped on an outcast. Because he was of mixed blood, other children of his own age would have nothing to do with him. But Ki and his mother had steadied themselves against the cruel barbs of being ostracized because they knew that their lives would be fulfilled in America. America, where people of all races came in the hope of equality and opportunity. America the beautiful, where who your parents were did not matter so much as what you could do with your own will and strength and determination.

Tragically, Ki's father had died of a blood disease just one month before they were to sail for America. There had been no one willing to protect them. His mother was, for all her noble blood, helpless against rival businessmen who had stolen all her husband's assets and money. She had tried to seek help, but her own family could not forgive her and her husband's family wanted no part of a Japanese woman and a grandson whose eyes were slanted and whose other features also reflected his Oriental heritage.

Abandoned, Ki's mother had soon died of a broken heart, and the five-year-old boy was turned away from every source of comfort because of his "impure blood." Ki remembered how, with his strength almost gone and his clothes in rags, he had found an old samurai without a master who was now forced to be called *ronin*. In Japanese, *ronin* meant a "wave man," one blown aimlessly like the waves of the ocean. Owning nothing, belonging to nothing, being nothing—that was *ronin*. That was Hirata, the giant with muscles like rocks and a heart like a mountain of sandstone. Hirata had tested him by trying to drive him away, but Ki had sensed one even lonelier than himself and in even greater pain. The old *ronin* had taken the boy in, and had treated him hard, but fairly. Taught him the ways of a samurai, not just how to fight but how to live and die, if necessary, with honor and dignity.

In their last years together, Ki and Hirata had grown to be closer than most fathers and sons. Hirata's words echoed still from that last day they were together: "In you I took the last true pupil. In you I have been able to turn the wheel of my life one complete cycle. Now that I have taught you all I know, you must go off to wherever your vow shall take you."

Ki had known that Hirata was ready to die and had

116

known better than to argue when the *ronin* had sent him away for a short while. When he had returned, Hirata was dead, the blade of his short sword buried to the hilt in his abdomen. Hirata had committed a perfect *seppuku*, ritual suicide.

Courage. Honor. Tradition. These were the things that a samurai held most sacred. These were the things Hirata had taught him. Jessica Starbuck was Ki's master—not legally, but in spirit, for he had dedicated his life to protecting her. And without a high and noble purpose in life, a samurai was nothing.

Ki must have dozed. It was sometime after midnight and the front door to the sheriff's office was opening. Ki wondered if Sheriff Colton's wife was over her fever. He should ask, but perhaps the man would prefer to be left alone to worry privately. Ki did not stir from his pallet.

He listened to the door open and then the sound of footsteps. He heard a match strike, and then the footsteps retreated back toward the doorway. The sudden light seemed brighter than necessary and Ki reached up to shade his eyes. That was when he heard the crash of breaking glass and the sudden whoosh of kerosene igniting across the wooden floor.

Ki jumped up and, half blinded by the sudden brilliance of the fire, he saw a man wearing a mask. The fire danced up between them, already eating hungrily at the boards and following the trail of fuel to the wall, where it climbed with a ferocious intensity.

The man stared through the smoke and flames at Ki and, over the roar of the fire, he began to laugh. His hands were on his hips and his hat was pulled low. Still, Ki could tell that the man was not Sheriff Colton. And when he turned to leave Ki to burn to death, the samurai reached inside his vest lining and pulled out a *shuriken* star blade. Ki hurled it with deadly force and it spun through the flames to lodge in the man's back. The assassin had been about to open the door, but now he sagged against it and knocked it shut. He staggered around and managed to get his gun out of his holster. Ki had another *shuriken* ready, but it was not necessary. The man pitched forward, firing down at the burning floor. He got off one bullet cleanly, but his body muffled the sound of the second shot.

Ki grabbed the cell door and shook it hard. He had a lock pick hidden in the lining of his vest like the one Jessie had used. But opening a simple hotel-room door was one thing; opening a locked jail cell was quite another. To complicate things, Ki would have to work from the back side of the lock. Ki glanced at the fire, knowing it was the poisonous smoke that would kill him long before the flames. One deep inhalation of the noxious fumes and he would be blinded and choking. A second and a third lung-ful of smoke and he would be dead within moments. The smoke was billowing up and filling the room at ceiling level. It was coming down fast and Ki cursed himself for not waiting to throw his *shuriken* blade after the man had opened the door. Even though the open door would feed the fire, it would also allow an exit for the smoke and attract help.

Ki worked furiously at the lock. His dark eyes reflected the flames that grew stronger with every passing second. The heat was already intense. His eyes were burning and, when he looked up, it was as if a great, poisonous cloud was dropping right down on top of him.

Ki dropped to his knees and lowered his head. His strong hands worked and the lock resisted. He began to cough. This caused him to lose control of the pick in his hand. He lost the feel of the locking mechanism. Ki shut his eyes and felt his hands and extremities begin to tingle. A terrible coughing spell dropped him to the floor. He pushed himself up and forced the pick back into the lock.

"Ki!" Jessie screamed. "I heard the shot. Ki!"

Somehow, she made it to the cell. He gave her the pick and she worked with a concentration that was unbroken until the door snapped open. Ki could smell hair burning and he hoped it was his rather than hers. He ducked his head and took a deep breath of the clean air that hugged the floor. When he reached for Jessie's hand, he found her almost unconscious on the floor.

"No!" he screamed, snatching her up and hurtling through the flames. The clear air outside struck him like a cold bath and he plunged into a horse trough. When he tipped Jessie's face up to his own and stared at her in the moonlight, he saw her eyes flutter open and she hugged him tightly. Ki was glad she could not see that his tears were mixed with the trough water. They both turned to watch the sheriff's office going up in flames. A fire bell began to toll just up the street and men came dragging a fire wagon.

"Sonofabitch!" Sheriff Colton cussed, staring as the roof of his office building collapsed and hundreds of men rushed in to keep the fire from spreading through the entire downtown. A bucket brigade was quickly formed and reached to the Truckee River.

"What happened?" the sheriff asked.

Ki accepted the sheriff's help in getting across the street. He sat Jessie down in front of the mercantile store. "You saved my life," he told her.

"How many times have you saved mine and helped me keep my Starbuck enterprises alive and safe from—"

Jessie stopped in midsentence, but it was already too late. The sheriff was not the only one hovering over them. Orin Grayson's shock and then fury was reflected in the firelight. It bronzed his face and made it as hard as that metal. Ki looked into Grayson's eyes and they were molten with hatred. Then Orin Grayson spun on his heel and marched down the street. He knocked a man aside as he cut through the bucket brigade and passed out of sight.

"What the hell is wrong with him?" Sheriff Colton asked. "One minute he was all upset because of Miss Wilson here, and the next—well, I never saw a man with a look in his eye like that unless he was ready to draw a gun and kill somebody. But Mr. Grayson, well, he's a state assemblyman and no man of violence."

Jessie and Ki exchanged glances. They knew how dead wrong Sheriff Colton really was. The time for game-playing was over.

Orin Grayson wanted to kill or get drunk, he wasn't sure which first. As he stomped down the street, he was trembling with rage and knew he was in no state of mind to go into a saloon. His nerves were on a hair trigger and he was spoiling for trouble. A thread of reason told him he had better go to the Sierra Stage Line offices and empty the bottle of whiskey he had in his desk drawer. He would drink until all the demons in him were weak and spinning, and then he would fall asleep on his couch. The couch where he had often sampled the womanhood of Roxy Bonaday and once, that of Jessica Starbuck. My God, how could he have believed a woman that smart and beautiful could have been some common hustler! Everything about Jessica Starbuck screamed that it was a lie when she said she was some poor, down-and-out cousin looking for a handout.

"She made a fool of me," Grayson muttered angrily. "Even when she was screwing me, she was probably laughing and trying to get those goddamn names!"

But he had not given them to her! Grayson reminded himself of that. It was a thin thread of victory, but one he would hang on to as he lowered himself into whiskey-soaked oblivion this night. He would have to kill Jessica Starbuck and that Chinese man who had twice escaped their hired killers. Jessica's half-conscious words to the Chinaman had only confirmed the conclusion Orin Grayson had reached when he saw the woman risk her life in the sheriff's office. He had watched them burst outside and had known instantly that those two were not strangers.

I need to think, he decided. I need to get drunk tonight, but then I need to get Lee Ford and sit down and plan how the hell we are going to do this thing once and for all. A stick of dynamite hurled through the Bonaday Stage Line office window while they were all inside? No, that would bring on an investigation. Much too risky and crude. Besides, with the luck he had been running today, something would go amiss. The dynamite fuse either wouldn't stay lit or else they would catch it and hurl it back out the window. Poison? A possibility. One thing for sure, he wanted them all dead now. Even Roxy.

Roxy had come to see him right after her father had died. She had been in tears and he thought she had needed comfort, but he'd been wrong. She had told him that she had promised her father not to see him anymore. At least not as long as there was a Bonaday Stage Line operating. When he had tried to change her mind and take her in his arms, she had become stiff and unyielding. His mistake was in trying to pull her down on the couch and make love to her. A stupid mistake; it had sent her into a rage. She had struck him and he had punched her without thinking. When she picked herself up from the floor in his office, her lips had been smashed and bloody. She had smiled and thanked him for showing her the truth. The bitch! The stupid . . .

Grayson stopped before the Sierra Stage Line offices and saw a light burning inside. He yanked out his pocket watch and saw it was one-thirty in the morning. He replaced his watch and his hand reached into his coat pocket to clasp the hideout gun he carried. Maybe the Starbuck woman had hired some detective to rifle the files in search of information.

Grayson crept up to the building and peered through the window. He saw nothing in the outer office, but light was coming from Lee Ford's little rat-hole space. Grayson moved inside and then slipped through the outer office with the gun pointed ahead of him. He was almost happy now. Catching a thief in the act would be a good excuse to kill and then get drunk, thus satisfying both of his urges.

"Bakemore?"

The bookish little accountant was sitting cross-legged on the floor with a lamp beside him. He was so engrossed in the ledgers spread out around him that Grayson had to repeat his name much louder. "Bakemore, what the hell are you doing in Mr. Ford's office at this time of night!"

The accountant jumped to his feet, spilling the ledgers and a file of letters and documents all over the floor. "Mr. Grayson!" he cried, "I . . . what are *you* doing here at this hour, sir?"

Grayson bent down and picked up a sample of the documents that lay scattered about. His eyes scanned them and he saw at once that they were mostly letters from their partners in Sacramento. Most of them were lengthy and damning. Each had been hand-delivered and they should have all been destroyed, or at least locked in the vault.

Grayson stiffened. Maybe they had been in the vault. It wasn't like Ford to leave this kind of evidence unlocked. The letters gave dates, events, and names of out-of-state outlaws hired to wage war on the Bonaday Stage Line.

Grayson swung around and walked over to the vault. The only ones who had ever opened it—until tonight— had been he and Lee Ford. He turned around slowly to look at the white and trembling face of Peter Bakemore. "The vault door is open a crack. Where did you find the combination?"

Bakemore wrung his hands. "I . . . ah, Mr. Grayson, sir. I really want to say that I have always been a good employee and I appreciate—"

"Answer me, you sniveling sonofabitch!"

"Please, Mr. Grayson. I just want to leave and go home now. I'll come back early and put everything in order and then I want to resign. I'm . . . I'm very sorry."

Grayson pulled the hideout gun from his coat pocket. It was a pearl-handled .22-caliber. "I'm sorry, too. She got to you, didn't she? Jessica Starbuck bought you. I thought you were incorruptible, but I was wrong."

"Please! I don't know what you mean!"

"Yes you do, Peter. Now back into Mr. Ford's office like a good boy. That's far enough."

Grayson stepped inside the littered little room. He closed the door, knowing that it and the outside door would effectively muffle all sound of gunfire.

"Good night, traitor," he whispered, pulling the trigger and watching the horror spread across Bakemore's thin, scholarly features.

"Oh, no!" the man screeched. "Please, Mr.—"

Grayson smiled and pumped three more bullets into Bakemore's narrow chest and watched him collapse across the scattered ledgers and papers. They would soak up the man's blood—that was all the records and pages of tabulations were good for anyway.

Orin Grayson closed the disgusting little office and walked back to his own neat, tidy one. After he lit a lamp on his desk, he selected a good brand of Kentucky whiskey from his liquor cabinet and a crystal glass. He shined an offending water droplet away with the cuff of his expensive shirt. Holding the glass up to lamplight, he inspected it carefully and then nodded with approval. He filled the glass with whiskey and lit a cigar, then settled back to think and get drunk.

He would have to request more men and money. The three financiers in Sacramento were not going to be pleased. Each day for the past week they had been expecting to receive a telegram telling them that the Bonaday Stage Line was bankrupt and its rolling stock could be picked up for a song. Now, he was going to have to tell them that Jessica Starbuck and a mysterious half Oriental who was either damn lucky or damn good were here to help the Bonaday kids. The three Sacramento men would be very unhappy about that, but it could not be helped. It was time that they realized the stakes had just gone up. Grayson would need at least a dozen gunmen to stop the Bonaday stagecoaches dead in their tracks.

He closed his eyes, feeling the warm heat of the whiskey begin to take effect. He did not want to remember how he had been made a fool of by Jessica Starbuck and how she had almost succeeded in learning everything about the operation. Had that traitorous fool, Bakemore, told her anything? Maybe, but maybe not. Either way, she and her

Oriental friend were as good as dead. If they stepped outside the Bonaday offices, they were easy targets. If they stayed inside, Grayson and Lee Ford would systematically bring the Bonaday line to ruin in very short order.

It did not matter. There was just one thing that he regretted, and that was that he could not kill Jessie personally. Roxy? Well, she was only a pawn, a foolish young woman with more spunk than good sense. And he had taught her a few things, hadn't he? Grayson smiled to remember how she had become an accomplished lover under his tutelage. Maybe she could be spared and . . .

Grayson rejected the idea. Lee Ford would not approve of sparing any of them. He'd want a clean sweep, a total elimination of them all. Better that way.

Grayson finished his whiskey, poured another, and lurched out of his chair. He could feel the whiskey taking effect after just one glass. He walked back over to Ford's office and studied the dead accountant's pathetic, crumpled figure. A wave of contempt and pity swept over him and he wheeled about and returned to his office chair. Bakemore had been one of that kind of men Grayson neither understood, or cared to. He had been totally committed to his ledgers and records, to neat little columns of unending figures. Everything had to be recorded. A man could always deny he said something, but he was a sucker and a goner if he had written evidence to go against him in court. I will have to talk to Ford in the morning about how we shall dispose of the body and of those incriminating files, he thought. Better to slip them out and bury—or burn—everything. Cremation. Neat and complete. Yes, he thought, with a nod of his head. That is what we will do with the man and his goddamn figures.

Grayson shook his head and drained his second glass in a single series of gulps. He wiped his lips and then his watering eyes with the white silk handkerchief in his coat pocket. He had a theory about the world that went like this: There were lions and sheep. If you were a lion, you were the king and you roared and took what you wanted. If a sheep got to thinking it was a goddamn lion, you slaughtered it so that all the other sheep would not make the same mistake. Peter Bakemore had most certainly been a sheep. But Jessie, though a woman, was a lion and so was her nameless half-Oriental friend.

When the lions did battle, the jungle shook and even the tops of the trees trembled. Grayson smiled because he was the biggest, meanest lion in Western Nevada. And this was his jungle to rule and to keep.

Chapter 11

"So that's it, huh?" Billy said, glancing at his sister. "The whole thing was a big lie cooked up by you, Ki, and my father."

Ki blinked. He was annoyed at this young fool for being so abusive. "What you don't seem to realize is that Jessie has put her life in great danger by trying to help your stage line."

"Well, you can both go back to where you came from!" Billy said angrily. "Roxy and I weren't in on this little game when it started, and we don't want any part of it now. Is that understood?"

Jessie was struggling with her own anger. She could understand why Roxy and Billy felt hurt and offended— after all, no one had trusted them to keep the secret. But had there been any reason to trust this pair? Billy had shown no sign of taking responsibility for his actions. He was a womanizer and a swaggering braggart. Roxy, well, she was sleeping with Orin Grayson and telling herself that she was love and they would be married.

"It's up to you," Jessie said. "We'll be on the next train out of here if you want, but I think you ought to use your brains instead of your heart before you say anything more."

"Your father ruined my father!" Billy shouted.

"The hell he did!" Jessie's green eyes were storming. "Have you already forgotten what your father's last words were? He said he loved Alex Starbuck and that my father won fair!" She looked at Roxy. "Do you remember that?"

Roxy was subdued and seemed very depressed. "Yes. And Father asked us both to trust you and let you help us. It was very, very important to him, Billy. It was about the last thing he said before he died."

Roxy took a deep breath and let it out slowly. "Billy, the last thing you did was promise our father that you were going to beat the Sierra Stage Line. That you were going to use your brains and your gun. You swore it to Father just before he died."

"I will use my gun, goddamn it!" Billy spun around to leave. "That part of my promise I'll sure as hell keep!"

Ki stepped into the younger man's path. "No," he said. "If you go over to the Sierra Stage Line offices in anger, you won't live to reach either Grayson or Ford. You'll be shot down in their yard. No court would rule it anything but self-defense. You'd be giving your life away for nothing."

"Out of my way!"

Ki stood his ground and waited. "Not until you cool down and agree to use what brains you might have. You promised to beat Grayson, now live up to that promise! It's time to be a man, Billy. Quit acting like some kid anyone can bait with a woman or a taunt."

Billy roared in angry frustration and hurled himself at Ki. Billy was three inches taller and twenty pounds heavier, but Ki stood rooted in place and gave not an inch. When Billy swung, Ki ducked and delivered a soft *tegatana* blow that caught Billy on the collarbone and spun him half around.

Billy's face went white with pain and his left arm and shoulder seemed paralyzed for a moment. He took a step back and lowered his head, then charged. Ki waited until the last instant. Then suddenly his hand caught one of Billy's outstretched arms by the wrist and brought it down sharply. He twisted the wrist and Billy cried out in pain as his momentum and Ki's hold flipped him into a complete

128

circle. Billy slammed into the wall and lay stunned.

Jessie went to get water and a damp cloth to revive Billy. He had a lot of courage but not much good sense. She hoped that Ki had changed that a little. Ki had acted correctly in keeping Billy from charging off to die.

Roxy stared at Ki as if he had used supernatural powers of some kind. "I never saw anybody fight the way you just did. Who, or what, are you?"

"I was trained as a samurai," he said quietly, adjusting his clothing and watching Billy start to recover. Ki turned and stepped outside. The stage yard was deserted. All the employees had quit and there were six horses and a couple of coaches left. Ki moved off toward the corral, not wanting his presence to provoke young Billy any more than it had already. He did not enjoy making anyone look foolish. Ki received no measure of stature or pride from such a victory. His only source of real satisfaction was in keeping his body in perfect working condition and keeping Jessie's body alive and healthy.

"Hey, wait a minute," Roxy said, as she followed him out to the corral. "How did you do that to my brother? He's bigger and stronger than you, and yet you made him look like a kid up against a man."

Ki shrugged. "Your brother must learn to be a man now or he will be killed very soon. I did not wish to humiliate him in there."

"You didn't," Roxy said. "He and I are both capable of doing that for ourselves. Billy hasn't made half the fool of himself that I've been making of myself these past six months or so. Can you imagine how I feel inside after being so wrong about Orin Grayson?"

Ki turned against the pole corral fence. He reached out and touched the livid, purplish bruise across her cheek. "Did Grayson do this to you?"

"Don't tell Billy or he'll go after Grayson no matter what."

"I won't tell him," Ki promised. "That would not serve our purpose."

"What is your purpose?"

"I am Jessie's friend and I help her accomplish the things that she needs to do," he said, not wishing to go into detail.

"You and she . . . do you . . . well, you know."

Ki divined her meaning. "No," he said, not feeling in the least bit offended. "Miss Starbuck and I are more like brother and sister."

"Brother and sister?" Roxy shook her head. "I don't know how any red-blooded man could be around that woman and feel brotherly. She even makes me look like a dowdy old laundrywoman. Her figure is better than mine and she's beautiful. I'm just sexy."

Ki had to smile at that because the description was right on the mark. "I noticed," he said.

"Yeah, I thought you did," Roxy added, studying him closely. "I never met a man like you. When I saw you the first time, I said to myself, 'Roxy, there is a rich partly Chinese boy, and he sure is pretty. Probably not very tough or strong, but nice-looking all the same. Probably a lot better educated and with table manners and everything. I'm a coarse old stone and he's a polished gem.'"

Ki shook his head. "That's not true. I am nothing special at all. I have nothing. I aspire to be nothing but what I am. It is my purpose in life to serve Jessica Starbuck. To fight battles for her and to win them. To live with honor and dignity. Always."

"My life doesn't seem to have a purpose," Roxy said. "I have been twisting circles in the wind my whole lifetime. The harder I try to do right, the worse I do wrong. You may not believe this, but Orin promised me that he would take care of my father. And I believed him and even thought I was in love with the man."

"Love is ever changing, and yet it flows like a river without a beginning or end. It just is."

Roxy's eyes misted a little. "I never heard anyone talk like you do, Ki. You are special! I want you and Jessie to stay. We've no right to ask, but I'm asking anyway."

130

"We will stay," he said. "Miss Starbuck would never leave you to face your enemies without help. And neither would I."

Roxy sniffled, momentarily overcome. "I wish I didn't have this big bruise on my cheek so I looked so ugly to you."

His fingers were long and supple. His fingertips stroked her cheek so tenderly that Roxy did not feel pain, but instead, a soothing pleasure. She swallowed, and had to clench her hands at her sides to keep from putting them around him. She was weak and he was strong. She had nearly lost all of her father's love and respect and now she stood humbled and ashamed. Ki seemed able to look right through her into the cracks and dirty places. She wanted to run and hide but she was afraid he might let her.

"Roxy," Ki whispered.

She was fighting away tears.

He gathered her hand in his own and led her toward the barn. When they passed inside, he closed the door behind them and they stood in filtered sunlight. A horse stomped and whinnied, expecting hay. A flock of pigeons fluttered into the air, then beat noisily around the interior of the barn to resettle on their roosts and coo softly.

Ki placed his arms around her and felt her tremble. He said, "I know that you feel like you are nothing. I have felt that way before many times. And you have been foolish, but who has not? Your heart is strong and you are good inside, Roxy. Your heart should be filled with happiness. It—and you—are beautiful."

Roxy sobbed gratefully and threw her arms around his neck. She clung to him as if he were her salvation and light. "I don't even know you and I love you already," she choked. "Isn't that stupid! Aren't I such a fool!"

"No," he told her as he gently picked her up and carried her over to a stall filled with fresh straw. He laid her down and said, "I will never marry, and when Jessie and I are done and your enemies beaten, we will leave."

She hugged him with desperation. "Maybe I can change

your mind." She kissed him on the mouth hard. "I can be very persuasive, Ki!"

"I'm sure you can, but no. You have been deceived and hurt enough already. I must be honest with you now."

"But—"

Ki placed his fingers over her lips. "I will only promise you this. When I leave, you will know without a doubt that you are beautiful inside and out. And more than that, Roxy. You will know that you are destined to love and be loved—always. This is my promise to you."

Her eyes glistened. "I'm trembling. Do you have this effect on all women?"

"No," he said with an amused smile.

"Ki, I want you to make love to me now. I want you to show me that Orin Grayson is not the only man I'll ever have who could satisfy my hunger and make me feel all woman."

"You are all woman, Roxy."

"Prove it to me. Please, Ki, prove it to me right now!"

Ki did not need any further entreaties. He reached down and unbuttoned her blouse and then lowered his mouth to her proud breasts with the pink nipples already hard with desire. Ki's tongue darted out and Roxy gasped. She arched her back and Ki listened to her heart pound and her breath quicken. Roxy moaned, a soft sound deep in her throat. She began to roll her shoulders from side to side as Ki gently nipped first one breast and then the other.

"Oh," she whispered, "you haven't even gotten my skirt off yet and already I'm hot and wet inside."

"Maybe I had better get to that little problem," Ki said, pulling away her skirt and then her pantalettes to reveal a dark, steamy mass of wet curls between her legs. He studied her with admiration. She was luscious-looking. Her waist was narrow and her hips flared out beautifully. Her thighs were satin-smooth yet firm and muscled. Ki's fingertips caressed them gently and they spread open, wide and eager.

He pulled away and stood up for a moment to undress.

When he loosened his pants, his manhood jumped out straight and so long that her eyes grew round with surprise. She reached up and grabbed his shaft and pulled him down beside her. Then, her mouth closed over him.

Ki threw his head back and closed his eyes, feeling her lips suctioning and her tongue laving his throbbing manhood. "I'm not going to be able to take this for very long," he said with a happy sigh. "Not long at all."

She rolled to her knees and her hair fanned over his crotch as she worked on him with obvious pleasure. Ki stroked her lovely hair and rocked back and forth, feeling the fire in him glow hotter and hotter.

When his hips began to quiver, Roxy pulled back and then placed her hands on his chest. She spread her legs on both sides of him and reclined on the straw. Then she grabbed his shaft in both hands and said, "You've got me hot already just thinking about this monster. Now show me how a man uses it on a woman like me!"

Ki was more than happy to demonstrate his ability. He knew that, despite her boldness, Roxy was afraid that Orin Grayson was the only man who could bring her to a climax. Ki wanted to prove that any man who cared to give as well as receive pleasure could satisfy her fully.

He lifted his lean, powerful hips over her and felt her hands guide his shaft into her hot, wet depths.

"Oh, Ki, it feels like a log inside of me!"

He chuckled, reached down and grabbed her knees, and pulled them both forward. This opened her even wider and he drove himself in to the hilt. Roxy's eyes grew wide and almost amazed for a moment, then they slitted like those of a contented cat when Ki began a slow, rhythmic stroking. She crossed her ankles at the base of his spine and used her thighs to match his thrusts with her hips.

The straw crunched under their weight and it smelled sweet and wholesome. Ki lowered his mouth and used it on first one breast, then the other. His rhythm never varied until he felt her fingernails begin to dig into the flesh of his back. Then, he looked into her glazed eyes and knew that

133

she was starting to lose control. Her breathing was coming in gulps and her hips were starting to jerk ever more violently. She was coming closer and closer to her moment and Ki knew he could bring her there whenever he wanted. He waited a little longer until she began to moan and thrash.

"Please, Ki, hurry with me," she begged. "I'm going crazy. I'm on fire!"

He quickened his thrusting and began to drive into her harder. She matched his strokes with fierce desire and their bodies grew wet and slick with perspiration and their love juices. Roxy tried to beg him again but she was almost incoherent and her lips moved soundlessly as her head tossed from side to side.

It was time. Ki had gone too far with a few women and driven them into a faint. He wanted this woman to stay aware every moment. "Now!" he grunted, letting his lean body loose itself from his mental control. His body began to slam in and out and Roxy's hands moved wildly across his back.

"Yes, yes!" she screamed. "It's coming, yes . . . ohhh, yes!"

Ki covered her mouth with his own and his mind soared into an explosion of ecstasy. Dimly, he felt the girl under him bucking and thrashing as his own body began to spasm with mighty convulsions. His hot seed filled her with great, driving spurts and it went on and on until he crested and there was nothing more inside of him to put into her.

Their bodies continued to rock and twitch for several exquisite moments. Then they lay still, gasping for breath and feeling their heartbeats gradually return to normal.

Roxy hugged him tightly. "Ki, I never, never believed it could possibly be so beautiful. So strong and soaring. I . . ." She shook her head. Her hair was wet and plastered to the edges of her face. She could not put into words how wonderful it had been.

"You have freed me from all my doubts," she whispered to him. "As long as you stay, I'm your love slave."

Ki laughed. "You underestimate your own powers. As long as I am around you, I won't be able to get enough of your womanhood."

He started to pull away but she gripped him tightly with her arms and legs and her womanhood. "Uh-uh," she whispered. "Stay right where you are. I want to see how fast you recover and how often I can use you as a stud."

"You're shameless," Ki said in a teasing voice.

"I know," Roxy replied, pulling his face to her breasts and wiggling them until he felt his desire start to rebuild. "And when I find a good thing, I make the most of it."

Ki could feel his shaft rapidly stiffening again. He would take her again before resting. Only this time, it would be even slower, more delicious than the last. He would discover exactly how long Roxy could circle around and around the lip of ecstasy without toppling over the edge.

Chapter 12

Jessie had sent a few telegrams the very same afternoon that Dan Bonaday had died. And now, as she read them, she nodded with encouragement. The Starbuck empire was widespread and extremely diversified. Jessie had mining interests scattered throughout the world, and several of them were in Nevada. Not that she always owned big mines outright, though that was often the case, but sometimes she owned just enough stock in them so that her interests were always of paramount importance to the board of directors. What she had asked Mr. Friendel was to provide her a list of the Nevada mining companies in which she currently possessed significant stock ownership.

The list she received by telegram included three names and one of them, the Jumbo Mining Company, bore a Reno address. Jessie had no difficulty whatsoever in locating its office and gaining an introduction to its president, Mr. Archibald Potter.

He was a talkative, potbellied man who was rumpled and relaxed and seemingly content with being in his sixties. he smoked a briar pipe that would not stay lit and whose chewed-up stem he used liberally to punctuate his sentences.

"My dear Miss Starbuck, this is a great honor!" he said after one of the office clerks escorted her into his small but comfortable office. "I once worked with your late father, and it was a high point of my middle years. Alex Starbuck was a man's man if ever there was one."

"How did you work together?" she asked, taking the seat that was offered.

"Many long years ago I was educated as a geologist. Your father, of course, was a brilliant seaman and entrepreneur. He was interested in mining and I had the great pleasure of showing him claims all up and down the eastern slope of these Sierras."

"I see."

"We overturned a lot of rock in the month we traveled together. You know, your father could have traveled like a king. He was rich enough, of course, but he insisted on traveling fast and light. We slept out under the stars. Ate jerky, beans, and sourdough biscuits, roughed it like a couple of old prospectors down on their luck. Nobody knew who he was and he wouldn't let me tell them anything, except his first name. 'Course, they never dreamed who he was or what he was worth. If they had, well, there are some desperate men crawling around out there in the deserts and hills."

"I know," Jessie said, deciding she liked and would trust this simple, straightforward man. If her father had been willing to trust his company and judgment, Jessie figured she could do the same. "Mr. Potter, I—"

"Archie. Please call me Archie. Everyone does."

"All right. Archie, I have a problem. I am trying to help another old friend of my father's. Actually, I should restate that to say, a couple of the descendants of an old friend."

"Who are they?"

"Bill and Roxy Bonaday, of the Bonaday Stage Lines."

"They still in business? I heard they went under the same day that Dan passed on."

"That's not true. They are being forced into insolvency by the Sierra Stage Line."

Archie expelled a deep breath. "I'll be honest with you, Miss Starbuck. Up until about four months ago, we did all

138

our business with Dan Bonaday. I liked the man very much. He was rough, but a man of his word. I trusted him. But then, it got so that Dan couldn't guarantee his shipments anymore. We lost several thousand dollars in gold, and when highwaymen took another Bonaday coach along with our entire Candelaria payroll, I had to switch companies. A man can't sustain those kinds of losses very long and stay in business."

"And you switched to the Sierra Stage Line." It wasn't a question. Jessie knew that the man had, for there was no other stage company in town.

"Yes, we did. Seemed the only thing we could do. I had heard the rumors that the Sierra Stage Line might be up to some skulduggery. But damn it, Miss Starbuck, I got my own company problems. I told Dan that when he asked me why I was no longer using his stage line. He got mad as hell and we had a few harsh words."

Archie shook his head. "Dan could get real hot and nasty. I just refused to deal with him. And I'll tell you this, every single shipment of gold or payroll has been delivered by the Sierra people since we gave 'em our business."

Jessie stood up. She looked out the window into the street without really seeing anything. "Archie," she said at last, "I understand your position—but I think you are wrong. The people robbing and sabotaging the Bonaday line were most certainly gunmen hired by the Sierra Stage Line."

"You can prove that?"

"No. But it stands to reason who had the most to gain. How many Sierra coaches were being robbed?"

"None."

"That's right. What is happening here is that once the Sierra line is the only one left, they'll jack their freight, bullion, and passenger charges sky-high. Over a period of one year you will be brought down to your knees. And if you try to do your own freighting, you'll suddenly have highwaymen all over your wagons. Archie, it doesn't take a lot of imagination to see that you, and others like you, will be hogtied over a barrel. I need your help to see that never happens."

Archibald Potter nervously relit his pipe. "What am I supposed to do?"

"Give the Bonaday line back your business."

The man shook his head doubtfully. "Miss Starbuck, I have to send twelve thousand dollars to cover a payroll down in Candelaria. Now that is about a hundred and eighty miles of the most godforsaken country you ever laid eyes on. The stage line will stop a dozen times at towns, outposts, and way stations. And in every one of them there is danger. Now I ask you, how could you possibly agree— as one of this company's major stockholders—to allow the Bonaday line to handle that kind of money, given their past history?"

"I couldn't," Jessie answered truthfully. "But there will be a few changes on this run. Namely, I and a man named Ki will be on this stage and nothing will stop us from delivering as promised."

Archie shook his head. "Miss Starbuck, the last time I lost the payroll, fifteen highwaymen attacked the Bonaday stage just a few miles south of Genoa. It would have required a small company of United States Cavalry to prevent that robbery. I certainly appreciate your bravery, but—"

"Archie, I will guarantee delivery. And if we don't get either your payroll through or the bullion back here safely, then I will make up the loss."

"You'd do that?"

"Gladly," she said.

Archibald Potter scowled. Clearly, he did not like the idea of Jessie putting her own money or life in jeopardy. "And there is nothing I can do to talk you out of this?"

"Nothing whatsoever."

"All right," he said, "I'll do it. With your guarantee, I've nothing to lose. Of course, I'd want that guarantee in writing—just in case you have a . . ." The older man was clearly embarrassed to put into words what they both knew he meant.

"Fatal accident?" Jessie supplied. "Of course I'll put it in writing. And you are correct to ask for it. I'm a stockholder and I would have thought you remiss in your duty not to ask for the guarantee in writing."

"A mere formality, my dear. Your life concerns me far more than the money, or even the gold you will be transporting in your strongboxes. I don't understand why you are going to this extreme risk."

"It is a matter of principle. We either allow people like Orin Grayson and Lee Ford to gain some measure of control over our lives and businesses, or we do not."

Potter nodded as he tamped his pipe. "You're Alex Starbuck's daughter, all right. Godamn it if you don't make me feel like buying a Bonaday stage ticket and a double-barreled shotgun to take along!"

Jessie laughed. "Some other time, Archie. This is one stage that will be booked solid. Besides me and Ki, both Billy and Roxy Bonaday are coming."

The geologist's lined old face grew very serious.

"You make it much too tempting for your enemies. One stick of dynamite, one bullet into the driver's head as he rounds a sharp curve, one of a lot of things and they have finished all of you off in the same murderous stroke. Wouldn't it be much wiser if two of you remained in Reno?"

"Maybe." Jessie winked. "But you don't lure an entire pack of wolves into your trap with a couple of measly spareribs, Archie. You send them the whole beef."

Billy Bonaday held the lines between the fingers of his left hand just the way he had been taught by his father. Dan Bonaday had never claimed to be a true reinsman, but he had been good, and Billy had tried to learn all he could from the man. Part of the skill of handling a six-horse team was in hitching them up properly. In Europe and back East, they hitched their horses up snug to the tongue of the coach or wagon. Farmers did it that way, too. But a reinsman knew better. He left his team hitched loose so that the breast straps and traces dangled and there was a lot of slack to play with between the driver and the horses. This allowed the driver to direct his team as a maestro guided his orchestra. Undaunted, he could send his lead horses racing into a hairpin turn while the wheel horses were still galloping straight ahead. This daring technique had been demonstrated to Billy when he was young enough to feel certain the coach would overturn and they'd all die. But the solid Concord coaches skidded around a turn and then straightened out to run true.

Billy could feel the tension among them all. He felt responsible for getting the coach through. The fact that they were carrying the Candelaria payroll of almost twelve thousand dollars made his mouth dry. Billy wondered why in God's name a smart businessman like Archibald Potter had ever entrusted so much cash to them. It never occurred to him that Jessica Starbuck might have actually guaranteed against the loss.

"Is everyone ready?" Billy asked.

Ki finished helping Roxy into the coach, though she needed no help. She smiled with appreciation for his thoughtfulness and she even blushed a little when Ki's hand strayed to the calf of her shapely leg. That was good, Ki thought; Roxy needed to know she was very desirable. Orin Grayson might have shown her how a woman could respond in bed, but he had done nothing to improve her self-image. Ki meant to change that as quickly as possible.

"Are you ready to roll, Jessie?"

She nodded. "Once we get out on the road, I might just join you and Billy up on top. Best seat on the coach, you know."

"I know," Ki said, closing the door and hopping up to take his place as shotgun guard. "Roll it, Billy. We have a long, hard road to travel."

"You don't know how hard," the young man said, snap-

142

ping the whip with his right hand. A real driver could pulverize a fly on the lead horse's head, but not Billy. He was content just to use the long, braided whip to keep the horses' attention.

As they rolled out of the Bonaday stage yard, Billy remembered a few years back when it had been a beehive of activity almost twenty-four hours a day. Back then, there had been a full crew of hostlers, drivers, and stablemen. There was a man to do nothing but unload the baggage and another to hitch and unhitch the teams. And over in the pole corrals, there'd always been fifteen or twenty fine horses ready and waiting.

Now the Bonaday stage yard was empty, run-down, and quiet. As they entered the street, people looked with surprise at Billy and the shiny coach he drove. Bonaday coaches hadn't been seen for a while and Billy guessed most folks figured the firm was busted. Well, he thought grimly, not quite. This is our last chance to prove we can cut it and play to win.

He drove down Virginia Street because it was busy and he wanted everyone in Reno to see Billy Bonaday driving his father's coach. A few people waved, and one even shouted to him, "Good luck!"

Billy tipped his hat to a pretty lady and made her blush when he stopped the coach dead in the street and blocked traffic just so the woman could cross. Someone bellowed in anger for him to get going, but Billy paid him no mind until the woman reached the far side of the street, turned, and smiled gaily at him, obviously flattered by his consideration.

Billy chuckled deep in his throat. He knew he made a handsome and rakish figure on the driver's seat of his own coach. He tipped his hat and drove on, feeling pretty good, until he passed the Sierra Stage Line yards. He slowed the team to a crawl but did not stop outright. Grayson and Lee Ford saw him coming and so did some of their gunslingers.

Grayson was bold. The state assemblyman strode out to the street, bowed to Jessie and Roxy, and called up to

Billy, "Drive real carefully, kid. There are a lot of pitfalls between here and the end of the line. We sure don't want anything to happen to those beautiful women. Keep your eyes open, Chinaman!"

Billy grabbed for the handbrake, but Ki clamped his fingers on the man's arm painfully hard. "Don't let him bait you into a fight now!" he hissed. "Don't you see that's exactly what he wants, with ten gunslingers standing behind him?"

"Why wait?" Billy choked. "You know that they're coming after us anyway. Let's settle this once and for all."

"Keep driving," Ki said tightly, "or I'll throw you to them and drive on myself. There is always a right and a wrong time and place and this is the latter. Now, do as I tell you!"

Ki rarely let his temper show but when it did, it came in such a way that a man took notice. It was not Ki's way to shout and make a fuss, he just warned a man one time and then let him choose the consequences. Looking into Ki's eyes, Billy suddenly realized that he did not want to force a confrontation. He wanted Ki with him, not driving away from a man he considered a headstrong fool.

"All right," Billy managed to say, pulling his arm free while he could still move his fingers. "We wait."

"Good," Ki said. "Patience is a virtue. You have made the first small step."

Billy wanted to tell him to go to hell, but he decided that would not be very smart.

The coach rolled on.

"Damn it!" Lee Ford growled, watching the stage disappear. "I'd have bet my ass that Billy would have stopped and we'd have forced the showdown."

"It was the Oriental," Grayson said. "Didn't you see how he controlled Billy? That man is extremely dangerous."

Ford nodded. "I think I'd better go along with our men this time just to make sure that nothing else goes wrong."

"Good idea." Grayson started to turn back toward the

144

offices, but then hesitated. He turned and walked back to Lee Ford, who was already preparing to ride. "Lee, wait until they get a hundred miles south of here, then hit them. Telegraph me as soon as it's done. And . . ."

"Spit it out, Orin!"

"All right. I don't care what you do to the men, but I want the two women to die cleanly. No raping, no rough stuff. Just a quick kill."

Lee Ford cocked the hat back on his head. Once, he had been a hired killer. It was hard to believe because of his weight, but it was true. He'd been a bounty hunter and a scalp hunter as well, and he was a dead shot.

"Orin," he drawled. "You get your tender ass back in a chair where it belongs and don't try to tell me my business. You already had both them women and you don't want any of us to do the same. I say horseshit to that noise. We'll do it our way and I already promised the men that we might have us a little pleasuring before we kill them women."

Grayson swallowed and headed back to the office without another word. Most people thought he was the ramrod of the stage line, but he wasn't. When it came right down to who was calling the shots, Lee Ford was the top dog. Lee Ford, who would kill him in a second and never think twice about it.

Grayson stopped at the front door of his office and watched the Bonaday coach disappear around a corner. It was Roxy he felt sick about. She hadn't done anything to deserve the fate that awaited her now. The other three could suffer and their souls burn in hell. But Roxy had loved him, really loved him, and Grayson wished things might have gone better. He could have married her, and he would have if it had not been for Lee Ford.

Damn Ford. Poor, trusting Roxy. She deserved a whale of a lot better end than she would receive. Lee Ford and his men had lusted after her for a long time.

145

Chapter 13

About ten miles below Reno they swung southeast and climbed the rugged grade up to Virginia City. The Comstock was on the decline but even so it still supported several thousand people. The Ophir and the Potossi Mines were still operating with reduced crews, but Ki thought the town had the look of death to it. Even so, Virginia City, Gold Hill, and Silver City were each grimly hanging on to their economic existence. Dan De Quill and Mark Twain no longer worked for the famous Territorial Enterprise, but the Delta and Bucket of Blood saloons were sure doing a whale of a business. Occasionally, a few passengers would climb aboard, but they were just out for a short haul. Since the Bonaday Stage Line had not maintained a regular passenger schedule for some time, the passengers seemed to have preferred either to wait for an oncoming Sierra coach or use their own sources of transportation.

Ki had never seen a harder country or people. The country itself was nothing but harsh, rocky mountains that had been completely denuded by the miners, who used every bit of timber either as underground shoring or firewood. Everywhere Ki looked he saw small mine tailings that gave evidence of where some luckless miner had busted his back in the vain hope of striking paydirt. The tailings were abandoned now, and even the big mines mostly stood empty with their huge gallows-like hoisting works and steam engines rusting in the sun.

"There's nothing sadder than a dying town," Billy said, reading Ki's thoughts. "Ten, twenty years ago you'd have had to pay thousands of dollars for each running foot of mining claim here in Six Mile Canyon. Why, my father said that men came from around the world to work these ugly hills. Well, they worked them, but old Sun Mountain yonder is still standing and the men are mostly gone now. 'Cept those buried here. A whole lot of them way down in mines so deep that the earth got hotter than hell to work in."

"Hold up there!" a man shouted as they approached a towering cut in the rock that the road passed through.

"Damn it!" Billy swore. "I'd a thought he would have given up on Devil's Gate Toll by now, what with everybody so poor they can barely feed themselves. But he hasn't. The greedy sonofabitch is still robbing anybody who'll let them."

Ki frowned. "You mean everyone who passes through this cleft in the rocks is supposed to pay him?"

"For a fact. He bought the rights to it ten, maybe twelve years ago. He's been bleeding people ever since. My father hated him. Everyone does. His name is Isaac Waltrop and he's tetchy as a teased snake. He's never been whipped and you can see from the size of him he's an ox."

"Then you'd better pay him and be done with it," Ki said. "We are transporting twelve thousand dollars in cash. This is not the time or the place to get into a squabble over a dollar or two."

"Maybe, maybe not," Billy drawled. "Last time I was through here he charged a poor widow and her three kids a dollar each. They didn't have it, so I paid their way. They were much too weak to climb far up into this mountain like you have to do to go around. I swore at the time I'd not pay Waltrop and his guards another penny as long as I live."

Ki lifted his glance upward and saw the pair of guards

148

with their rifles in their hands. They stood on opposiste sides of the cleft and each had a perfect firing angle down onto the narrow roadway. Between the huge, bearded Waltrop and his guards standing high overhead, Ki could certainly understand why people had little choice but to pay the toll. Still, it also grated Ki to have to submit to highway robbery. This was obviously a natural defile in the rocks, not some cut that Waltrop or any other human being had sweated and toiled to open for traffic and a reasonable return for their time and labor.

Waltrop was carrying a shotgun of his own and it looked like a toy in his fists. "Hold that stage up there, damn you!"

Billy pulled on the reins and the stage came to a halt. Ki could see that Billy was measuring the chances he had of getting through without paying. They weren't good at all.

"We'll pay him," Ki said. "I've got the money."

"Sure," Billy gritted. He reached out for the money and snatched it from Ki without thanks. "Waltrop, how much do you think you can rob me of this time?"

"Billy Bonaday, I guess you ain't learned any manners since the last time you was through, have you, boy?"

"Not a single damned one I can think of when dealing with a greedy pig like you."

Waltrop snarled and his deep-set eyes pinned Ki. "What's the matter, your stage line so poor you can't even pay a white man to be your shotgun?"

Billy flushed with anger.

"Easy," Ki whispered.

"Chinaman, put that shotgun down in the boot nice and slow before you accidentally shoot yourself. You yellow bastards ain't allowed to carry a man's weapon through Devil's Gate Toll."

Ki laid the weapon down. Between his legs and hidden in the front boot of the stage was his samurai bow. It was unusually shaped, and made of light-colored wood sandwiched between layers of dark. The wood had been fire-tempered until its flexibility, lightness, and strength were superior to any bow that could be found in the world, including those of the American Indian. Ki was an expert with the weapon and had often demonstrated that he could fire it with incredible speed and accuracy. A quiver filled with arrows lay within easy reach. Still, Ki did not believe he would use force unless it was required. He tolerated insults no better than any other man, but he had the self-discipline to know that getting the Jumbo Mine Company payroll through was all-important.

Waltrop stuck his fist up toward Billy. "Ten dollars because you got such a smart mouth."

"Ten dollars! You only charged me three the last time. I won't pay it!"

"Sure you will. 'Course, if you ain't got the toll, maybe one of your pretty lady passengers inside will help you out." Waltrop swung around and grabbed the door handle of the coach with a leer on his face. "Ladies, step down here and—"

Ki heard the familiar cocking sound of Jessie's gun and her whisper that carried a deadly warning: "Drop your shotgun, mister, and do it right now."

Waltrop dropped it and started to yell for help, but Billy sprang from his seat, landed on the giant, and knocked him flat. Ki grabbed his bow and an arrow, knowing that his shotgun would not be effective if the guards above began to fire their Winchesters.

A guard did lever a shell into his rifle and try to take aim, but the other one yelled, "Let 'em fight, you goddamn fool, you might hit the boss!"

The man lowered his rifle and waited for a clear shot at Billy.

"The boss will tear his head off anyway," the other guard said.

Ki had pulled his bowstring back to his ear and would have shot the guard if he had not lowered his weapon. Now, Ki turned his attention to Billy and winced as the young man took a roundhouse punch that lifted him clear off the ground and sent him smashing into the rock wall.

Their team of stage horses began to prance around and Ki grabbed the reins.

Billy didn't have time to notice. He had thrown his arms around Waltrop, trying to clear his head. The big man broke his locked arms and hurled him back against the rock wall. He grabbed Billy by the collar and measured him with his cocked right fist. But when he drove it at Billy's handsome face, Billy ducked.

"Owwwh!" Waltrop bellowed as his massive fist broke itself against the rock wall.

Billy was on him like a cat. Taking advantage of the blinding pain Waltrop had caused himself, Billy drove three punches to the giant's face and then made his cheeks billow out with a murderous uppercut to the heart.

Waltrop staggered, then charged Billy, but he was too slow and missed. As he passed, Billy punched him in the kidneys and Waltrop collapsed on one side. Billy smashed the giant twice more with solid blows that sent Waltrop backpedaling.

Ki was impressed. Billy had gained the advantage as much because of his cool thinking as he had his speed and fighting skills. A man who could fight with cool precision instead of just windmilling his punches and kicking and gouging was a man who could be counted on to maintain his composure under fire.

"Damn you!" Waltrop cried. He kicked out and Billy grabbed his foot and twisted it hard. The giant dropped in the dirt and rolled onto his back.

"Get up," Billy said, his face unmarked and his breathing still almost normal.

But Waltrop had taken all the punishment he intended to receive. Cradling his broken hand, he looked up to his guards and shouted, "Kill him!"

Ki drew his bowstring and fired in one smooth motion. Even before his arrow sped to its target, he was notching another in the desperate hope that he could take the second guard before the man killed Billy.

But there was no time and, when Ki heard the sharp

bark of Jessie's .38, he knew that he would not need another arrow.

The two guards were down. Ki could see neither of them, but he knew that both were writhing in agony from their wounds. His arrow had not been meant to kill, and he was sure that Jessie had not intended her shot to either.

Waltrop lay sprawled out on the dirt looking stunned at this sudden turn of events. In all of his years as tollgate owner, he had believed that his natural rock tollgate was invulnerable given the two guards he paid to stand watch from above.

In a fit of rage, he threw himself toward the shotgun he'd dropped in the dirt. Billy waited until he grabbed it and then stomped with the heel of his boot. Waltrop screamed and Billy pried the shotgun from his smashed fingers. Now the man had both hands out of commission. Billy pitched the shotgun up to Ki and said, "After the way you handled that bow and arrow, I know you won't need an extra, but I might before this trip is finished."

He climbed back up to the stage and tossed the money that Ki had given him down to Waltrop, who was moaning with both his bleeding hands held up before his ugly face.

Billy said, "The money is for your shotgun. We'll charge you nothing for the lesson you and your guards just received in manners."

Billy took the reins from Ki and leaned out over the coach. "Are you ladies all ready to roll?"

When Jessie and Roxy called up that they were, Bill Bonaday cracked his whip and they rolled on down toward Carson City.

Carson City was the capital of Nevada and a pretty town of about two thousand. At the eastern edge of the city, the Virginia and Truckee Railroad had built a major railroad repair shop called The Roundhouse. Billy drove past it to the main street of town and they passed the U.S. Mint and City Hall. A few blocks farther down they saw the impressive sandstone capitol building and then the Ormsby

House, where Billy pulled the team in and announced it was necessary to buy fresh horses.

"These are played out and need a couple of days' rest. We can use them on the way back."

Jessie nodded. "And I imagine you need to buy six good horses."

Billy smiled. "You got it figured just right," he said with a smile as he pulled out the pockets of his Levi's. "As you can see, I am plumb run out of money. And to tell you the truth, we can buy six horses here at a fair enough price, but it's going to cost you a bundle for another team when we have to change again in Candelaria for the trip back."

Jessie was a rich woman, but she did not like to have her money taken for granted or her renowned generosity to be taken advantage of. Her father had always believed that, since nothing in life was free, pure charity was a mistake. Make your gift cost the recipient something, no matter how small. Make them have a little something at stake too, or they'd soon get used to expecting something for nothing.

"Then I suppose you would like to sell me shares in your stage line?"

Billy's smile melted. "It's always been one hundred percent owned by our family. Be a shame to change that now."

Jessie shrugged. "You need a strong line of credit if you have any hopes of competing for new business or that U.S. Government mail contract Grayson told me about. What are you going to use for money if you refuse to sell me shares of stock?"

Billy thumbed his hat back. "I figured to use the money that old Archibald Potter will pay us for delivering his payroll to Candelaria and his gold back to Reno."

Jessie shook her head. "All right, the gentleman will pay you what the going rate of your competition is right now. The Sierra Stage Line would have done the job for three hundred and fifty dollars."

"Then I'll do it for two hundred and fifty!" Billy sputtered angrily.

"You will do it for three hundred," Jessie corrected him. "Always remember to beat the competition, but only a little. If you drop way below your competitor, instead of being thankful, the customer will jump to the conclusion that you've been making way too much money on previous deals. That makes him angry. If you have to beat a price, do it, but don't beat yourself in the process. Anyone can underbid his competitors and get the work, but you can go broke that way about as fast as any I know."

Billy did not look pleased at having been lectured. "Problem is, Miss Starbuck, you know way too damn much for your own good. I don't like women telling me how to run my business."

Jessie had dealt with a lot of fools, but this one topped them all. "It isn't your business!" she snapped. "At least not all of it. Roxy is half owner and, if you need to buy a couple of fresh teams of replacement horses, I'm going to own part of the Bonaday Stage Line too. Now, which are you going to listen to, your pride or my hard-earned advice?"

Roxy was listening and now she stepped forward and said, "We're going to listen to your good advice and take your generous offer of funds." She stuck out her hand. "Jessica, having you as a partner will give our stage company instant credibility and cash. Billy and I are damned grateful to you, Jessie. Aren't we, Billy?"

In answer, Billy ripped the Stetson off his head, slammed it into the dirt, and stomped it flat. "Yeah," he gritted as he strode away, "we are just plain overcome with joy!"

Roxy smiled and watched him go into the hotel. She shook her head and told Jessie, "He has always been a stubborn sonofagun, but he grows on you if you give him the chance. He'll come around and grow up one of these days."

Jessie nodded, remembering the fight at Devil's Gate Toll. "I'll at least say this much for your brother—he isn't afraid of trouble."

154

"Neither are you or Ki," she said.

Their trip on down to Mormon Station was uneventful. Jessie and Roxy both climbed on top of the rocking Concord coach and enjoyed the fresh air and the magnificent snow-capped mountains along whose eastern base they traveled. The country was beautiful, one long verdant valley after another. Mormon Station had been renamed Genoa and was right in that transitional period of its history where some people called it one name and some the other. It was the oldest settlement in Nevada, and one of the richest farming areas in the state.

The Mormons had settled and farmed it for many years, but had suddenly been called back to Utah by Brigham Young. When they had tried to sell out, no one had offered them a cent and they had left their lands, but many had burned their buildings rather than allow them to fall into the hands of those who had been unwilling to pay for them. According to Roxy, the departing Mormons had put a curse on this lush valley, prophesying that the winds would blow hard and incessantly. Maybe their curse had worked, for a strong wind was blowing that otherwise fine day.

"How far is this stage going south?" a middle-aged man who introduced himself as Austin Higby inquired when they arrived.

"All the way to Candelaria. But we weren't taking passengers from here south."

"But you must! I . . . I am more than willing to pay the fare, whatever it might be."

"Mr. Higby," Jessie explained, "the reason we don't want to take on passengers is that we are expecting trouble. Highwaymen."

He looked up at Ki. "The shotgun guard looks capable. Besides, I am a crack shot and well armed. I need to go south, Miss . . . ?"

"Starbuck."

"Miss Starbuck. It would be wonderful to accompany two such beautiful women and possibly to be of service."

155

"Suit yourself," Roxy said. "The fare is seventeen dollars to Candelaria."

"Seems a little steep," Higby said with a frown, "but I will pay it."

Roxy took the money and used it to buy them their dinner. As they were leaving, a tough-looking man of Higby's age said, "I believe I will ride along as far south as the boomtown of Aurora."

Roxy explained the danger this time, but the man just shrugged. He patted the gun at his side and smiled. "I'm used to trouble of all sorts. I was once a sheriff and then a range detective. I believe I can be of service, too." He introduced himself by the name of J. C. Long. "'Jesus Christ!' my father cried out when he first saw me. 'Ugly damn kid, ain't he!'"

Long smiled painfully at his own joke because he was exceedingly homely. He was a tall, thin man with a horse-face and slightly crossed eyes. He chewed tobacco and his teeth were badly stained. He smelled as if he had not had a bath in months. Both Jessie and Roxy wished he had not paid the fare but, seeing as how they had allowed Higby the choice of coming or not, they could hardly refuse Mr. Long. Jessie noticed that the two men hardly even nodded a greeting to each other. It seemed obvious that Higby disapproved of this odiferous and slovenly new traveling companion. But no one said anything. J. C. Long was another gun. And that might spell the difference.

So they careened out of Mormon Station, heading for the towns of Ludwig, Pine Grove, Rockland, and then Aurora and finally Candelaria. At each one, Jessie knew that danger awaited. But somewhere behind them—possibly even in front of them by now—was a gang of outlaws sent by Orin Grayson to stop this coach and end the game once and for all.

Between each town lay nothing but empty high desert. There were a thousand places where this coach could be attacked by surprise. Billy alone had covered the route to

156

Candelaria and, because of that, he was probably the most worried of all.

The night passed slowly, and morning found them bowling into Pine Grove. They were all weary and hungry. Pine Grove was a refreshingly attractive mountain village with a blacksmith shop, assay office, saloons, and boardinghouses. A stamp mill ran night and day, and its heavy pounding and steam engines made a frightful racket. Their horses were stumbling with fatigue.

"These won't make it to Candelaria," Jessie said after she disembarked. "We can't afford to have ourselves jumped by outlaws and have our horses too tired to run. Billy, if you can find another team of animals, I'll pay for them."

J. C. Long interrupted. "Excuse me," he said loudly in order to be heard over the stamp mill, "but I do know this town and its people. There is a livery down at the other end and I know the owner. I would, for two dollars, introduce you and put in a good word."

"Fine," Jessie said, paying the man. "It will be worth the money."

J. C. Long and Billy drove the exhausted team on down the street while Jessie, Ki, Roxy, and Higby went inside a small restaurant to order coffee and breakfast.

The food was not good but it was filling, if you didn't mind salt pork and burned flapjacks. They kept expecting Billy and Long to return, but there had obviously been some kind of delay.

"I had better go see if I can help," Ki offered, rising from his table.

"I'm sure they will be right back," Higby said.

But Jessie shook her head. "Why don't you go on and check anyway, Ki. Tell Billy that we have saved him some breakfast and that one cup of this coffee is about all anyone's stomach lining could stand."

Ki arose and left. He moved down the street quickly and, when he came to the livery, he saw their stage standing in front without horses. Ki looked around and saw no one. The corrals were almost empty except for their six lathered horses, which were standing with their heads down drinking fresh water.

"Billy?"

There was no answer, so he pulled open the door of the barn and stepped inside. At first he saw nothing, because his eyes needed a few moments to adjust to the dimness.

"Get him!" a man screamed.

Ki felt a rush of bodies. He kicked out blindly with his foot. He scored and a man grunted with pain but two more carried him down. The butt of a pistol smashed against Ki's head. Men pinned him down and their combined weight made it impossible to fight. Ki felt them roll him over on his stomach and then his arms were twisted around behind his back and tied brutally tight with a piece of wire.

Another fist sent an explosion of fire mushrooming up inside his skull. He lay still and fought to remain conscious.

"I told you there was twelve thousand dollars in that strongbox! Grayson sent me the telegram and I got it just before they arrived."

Ki recognized the voice of J. C. Long. So, he was in with them.

"What do we do next?"

Long chuckled. "Now comes the real fun part. We wait until the women come looking for these two and then we grab them and hold them for Lee Ford and his boys to do what they want."

"Are the women young and pretty?" a man asked eagerly.

"They are rosy and ripe!"

The men laughed obscenely. Ki gritted his teeth and began to struggle ever so slightly with the wire that bound his wrists. He knew everyone's life depended on his warning Jessie before she and Roxy stepped through that barn door—and that, hands bound or not, he was going to do his best to even the odds.

Chapter 14

Jessie had waited long enough. Something was wrong. Over the years, she and Ki had worked so closely and survived so many dangers together that they had each developed almost a sixth sense that warned them whenever something was seriously amiss.

Jessie arose from her chair and paid the breakfast bill. "They should have been here by now," she said, not wanting to alarm either Roxy or Higby. "I'll just go along and pull them back to their breakfast."

"I'm coming with you," Roxy said, knowing Jessie well enough to sense that she was trying to hide her concern.

Before Jessie could protest, Roxy was on her feet and moving toward the door. Higby started to rise but Jessie said, "No, this place is busy and I paid for those two breakfast plates. If you'll stay and watch over them I'll make sure that Ki and Billy eat before we leave. They have to be very hungry."

Higby frowned. "Are you sure?"

"Yes. Please wait and we'll all be right back."

"Okay," he said, lighting up a cigar and settling back in his chair. "In that case, I guess I'll have one more cup of that coffee."

Jessie forced herself to smile. "You'll be sorry, but go ahead."

She hurried after Roxy and when she caught up with her outside, she said, "Something is very wrong. Ki would never disappear like this without being in trouble."

"Maybe he and Billy had to go riding out in the hills to look at some replacement horses."

"That is possible, but I think they'd have ridden by and told us if they'd expected it to take very long."

Jessie and Roxy were both traveling in comfort and wore tight Levi's, cotton blouses, and soft denim coats. Because they expected trouble from the Sierra Stage Line's hired outlaws they each wore gunbelts and Colt revolvers on their shapely hips. Jessie was fast and accurate with hers, but Roxy had admitted that she missed as often as not.

Jessie studied the livery at the end of the street. She could see that the team of horses had been unhitched from the coach and that there was no one in sight. "It looks like a setup to get us in there," Jessie said. "Why don't you circle around behind and come in the back way shooting. Just be careful that you don't accidentally hit Ki or Billy."

"What if there isn't a back door?"

"There has to be," Jessie said. "But if not, tear off a board or shoot through a knothole—I don't expect you to kill anyone. Just get their attention so that when I come in the front door they'll be turned around and caught by surprise."

Roxy nodded and ducked into an alley. Jessie gave her five minutes and then she started for the livery barn. The street was dusty, flies swarmed in the morning sunlight, and a knot of men stopped talking in front of the bank to watch her pass by. One of them whistled softly in admiration and the others chuckled. Jessie did not even hear them.

Suddenly, she saw Roxy dart behind the barn and, in less than ten seconds, reappear with her thumb upraised. Jessie took that to indicate that there was a back door.

She stopped at the empty Bonaday coach and peered up

into the driver's boot. The strongbox was gone and that did not surprise her even a little. Jessie waited, pretending confusion. She gawked around as if searching for someone to help her find Ki and Billy. She was just fifteen feet from the huge barn doors and she swore that she could feel men staring at her through the knotholes.

Gunfire exploded in a short volley behind the barn. Jessie spun around and charged the doors. She grabbed a handle and pulled one open, then hit the ground and released two shots.

Ki was on his feet and moving. His wrists were bleeding badly from wire cuts and still tied behind his back. Yet his feet were unencumbered and they were at least half of his arsenal in the art of *te,* or empty-hand fighting. Ki's foot swept up in a vicious flat-footed kick that landed squarely in the groin of J. C. Long and dropped him. Ki saw Roxy shoot one outlaw point-blank, then disappear just before the other outlaws unleashed a hail of bullets. Ki moved swiftly to the attack. He drove his knee into a second man and, when two others realized that he was among them, Ki used a series of wicked lotus kicks that knocked them unconscious.

Jessie's gun blazed and the last of them standing died. J. C. Long tried to raise his gun, but Ki's foot broke his wrist and sent his weapon spinning. Long howled in pain and staggered out the front door.

"Let him go," Jessie said as she watched the man run down the street.

Ki revolved in a full circle, his eyes taking in the carnage they had wrought upon this band of outlaw gunmen.

He looked at Jessie, whose gun was sweeping over the ones that Ki had used his feet to disable. "If you'll untie me," Ki said, "I think we had better collect Billy, the strongbox, and the Jumbo payroll and then get out of here fast. From what I overheard, Lee Ford and many more are coming."

Roxy stepped into view. Once she was sure that Ki and

Jessie were alive and in control, she holstered her gun and hurried to Billy. Without a sound, she began to untie and remove her brother's gag.

The gag had been unnecessary. Billy was out cold. "He's been pistol-whipped from the looks of it," she said. "Big gash on his head."

Jessie quickly unwrapped the wire that bound Ki's hands behind his back. "Damn them!" she choked, clearly upset by his bloody wrists. "Look what they did to you!"

"I did that to myself by trying to break free," he admitted a little sheepishly.

"That was sure enough foolish!"

"Even I make mistakes sometimes," Ki admitted, knowing that she was deeply distressed for the pain he had endured trying to work free in order to save her from harm.

As soon as his wrists were free, he headed for the corrals to get six fresh horses. Billy was going to be no help at all in harnessing a team to the coach. It was a job that Ki did not look forward to but knew he could accomplish—and fast. J. C. Long or one of these other outlaws who lived to tell the story would let the word out that there was twelve thousand dollars cash in the strongbox. That kind of money might even attract them some unhealthy competition.

Ki and Jessie both had the same idea. They had to get the money and Billy and roll on toward Candelaria. If Billy was hurt badly, they could get him a doctor in the next town. But this one was unhealthy, and if Ki never saw Pine Grove again, it would be all too soon.

"Here, let me help you harness that team, Ki."

Ki looked up to see Austin Higby. "Do you have any idea where this strap goes?"

"Right here," the man said, taking it from Ki and attaching it to the traces. "This stuff is pretty tangled up. Somebody must have yanked it off the last team in a hurry."

Ki straightened up. He had rigged the harness together

162

as fast as he could, knowing that some of it was attached incorrectly. Ki did not greatly concern himself about that fact. As long as the main pieces of harness were in place and the tongue of the Concord was running down the middle, Ki figured that these horses could pull the stage without difficulty. Now, he watched with interest as Higby quickly reset straps and buckles. Ki was pleased to see that he had made very few errors. It took Higby less than five minutes to get the lead team in place and the reins running up to the driver's seat.

"Where'd you learn all about this?"

Higby smiled. "Been living out West all my life. A man without an honest trade will try anything to keep his belly full. I was once a hostler for Wells Fargo. Drove a little, too."

"If you are asking to take a turn, I wouldn't mind some help. Billy is hurt. He got his head cracked open and I think his ribs are also busted."

Higby nodded. "How many thieves did you have to kill?"

"Four. There are that many more still inside and disarmed. They'll be coming around soon enough. Rather than strike them again or go to the trouble of tying them up, Jessie and I would just as soon leave."

"Aren't you worried about them riding after you?"

Ki thought about how he had struck each man. "They won't be able to go anywhere this day," he said. "And by tomorrow, we will be in Candelaria."

Higby shook his head. "You really must be something with a gun."

Ki said nothing. It was against the samurai code to brag or in any way reveal his fighting secrets. All he said was, "Jessie and Miss Bonaday did their share, too."

Higby nodded. "I'll drive," he decided out loud. "But I expect to get a refund on my stage fare."

Ki had to work not to smile. "I think that sounds very reasonable, Mr. Higby. I'm sure we can arrange to refund your money."

"Good. Then let's get rolling before those birds inside come flying out of the barn or some of their friends decide to up the ante."

Ki nodded. "All aboard," he said, opening the door and helping the women lift Billy inside the coach and lay him out on the front seat.

"Put the strongbox in here with us," Jessie said.

"Sure," Ki answered, carrying it to the coach to place it on the floor. "They broke the padlock."

"So I see." Jessie reloaded her gun. "If they try for it again, they'll have us to contend with. And Roxy here is a much better shot than she gives herself credit for."

Roxy blushed. "You just take care of yourself up there, Ki."

Her hand lingered on his forearm and he felt her fingers tremble. They were eager for each other in lovemaking and Ki hoped they had the opportunity to sleep together for a night in Candelaria.

"Roxy, Mr. Higby is willing to drive us on to Candelaria if we refund his fare."

"Did you tell him we are in grave danger?" Jessie asked.

"He knows the situation."

Roxy reached into her purse and extracted the money that Higby had paid her before he boarded at Mormon Station. "I guess I'm the only one able to authorize Mr. Higby's refund. Here, give the man his money and express our appreciation."

Ki took the money and then climbed up onto the driver's seat beside Higby, who had the lines and was clearly ready to go. "Here's your seventeen dollars."

Higby stuffed it into his coat pocket without a word and cracked his whip with authority. The fresh team of horses threw themselves into the traces and the coach jolted forward, gathered speed, and raced out of Pine Grove.

Ki twisted around and looked back at the little mining town. Beyond it and to the north the way they had come

164

was a growing dust cloud on the horizon. Was it Lee Ford and his army of outlaws?

Ki turned back around and looked ahead to the south. A man could drive himself crazy thinking it was all sorts of things. When he was a boy living in Japan under the old *ronin*, Hirata, Ki had learned the value of not worrying about things over which he had no influence or control. Lee Ford and his men would come as surely as this day's sunset. And when they did, Ki would then be called upon to protect Jessie, Roxy, and even this stranger beside him willing to risk his life for seventeen dollars.

But until that time, it was pointless to worry. So Ki just made sure that his bow and arrows were ready, the shotgun was loaded, and the *surushin* rope with its small leather-covered steel balls at each end were tied neatly around his waist. He knew that Jessie would be thinking about every possible avenue of attack and defense. With fresh horses, they might actually be able to outrun any pursuit. In that case, trouble wouldn't arrive until the return trip to Reno. Ki smiled. That was at least two days from now. A lifetime if used properly.

Lee Ford and his body of fifteen proven gunmen arrived in Pine Grove just in time to see the doctor and the mortician attending their new clients. Lee dismounted heavily, then handed the reins of his lathered mount to one of his riders.

He stepped into the murky darkness of the livery barn and stared in disbelief at the sight of his men lying dead and wounded. J. C. Long had been his best gunmen, but he was finished for good this time. Some of the other men were strangers to Ford, but he knew that they had been first-rate, or they would not have been chosen and paid for by the three major owners of their stage line who lived in Sacramento.

He walked over to one of the injured and knelt beside the man. "Frank, I want to know exactly why you failed," he rumbled. "No goddamn excuses, just the facts."

The man was still in agony with crushed testicles tha were the result of Ki's sweep-lotus kick. Speaking betwee clenched teeth, he described the events to Lee Ford a clearly as he remembered and ended by saying, "I neve saw anything like that Chinaman, Lee. His hands were tie behind his back and he still swept through us like a sickl blade."

"But the women were the ones that shot the others?"

"Yeah. Billy was ours when they burst inside here Roxy Bonaday killed Everett first shot she took. Bob Hoy was next. About the time we got our guns out, the othe woman was firing from the front door. Between bein caught in their cross fire and that sonofabitchin' Chines killer, we didn't have a chance. We thought trappin' Bill was going to make the rest easy. You shoulda told us wha the other three could do."

Lee Ford scrubbed his face and asked the question tha had been troubling him most of all. "What about Austi Higby? Where was he when all this fun was going on?"

"Damned if I know. That yellow coward stayed out o the fight, damn his hide! Why, he even drove the Bonada stage out of here!"

Lee Ford stood up and, for the first time, he allowe himself a thin smile. "Higby is the only one of you wh has any brains. They think he's their friend now. He' going to set everything up for us in Candelaria. Higby i the key to the surprise I have in store for them. He's goin to make it possible to have it all."

"You mean the Jumbo Mine payroll and the bullion?"

Lee Ford nodded. "If we can get there before they d and set it up right. But either way, we'll finish this an come out rich and without a single competitor."

The man grinned weakly. "I'd sure like to see that, Lee Honest I would, but with each of my balls swollen up th size of apples, I can't ride a horse."

"You don't need to. Coming along right behind us is Sierra coach. You and nine other men will intercept th

Bonaday stagecoach after it starts back north with its load of bullion."

"Damn, that's a hell of an idea! No one would think to look inside for us after we steal that much gold. But I thought you said—"

Lee Ford cut him off with a contemptuous snarl. "Don't think, Frank. That's always been your problem. Just be ready when our stage comes along later this afternoon. And next time, no mistakes. Not unless you want to join J. C. and the other boys in Boot Hill."

Frank licked his lips and cradled his balls. He tried to smile, but his heart wasn't in it. He tried to think who was more dangerous, the Chinaman or Lee Ford. Ford, he decided. The Chinaman had won because he had surprised them with whatever kind of fighting he'd done. But kicks and such were no match for a single bullet. And that was what the Chinaman, or whatever he was, would get next time. The man was as good as buried already.

Chapter 15

They rolled into Candelaria late in the afternoon, and Jessie figured she had never seen a more desolate-looking town. It possessed nothing whatsoever of beauty except for its name, which meant "candle mass" in Spanish. Given that name, a newcomer might think that here, at long last, was a mining town with some spiritual awareness. That same visitor would have searched in vain for a single church of any denomination. Conversely, Jessie counted no less than twenty-five saloons, and every one of them was packed by miners either going on a shift or coming off one. Situated in a barren valley and surrounded by black lava mountains, Candelaria was a testimony to the willingness of men to live anywhere there was gold or silver waiting to be rooted out of the earth.

The streets were wide and filled with ore wagons and foot traffic. As the Bonaday coach rolled in, men waved from the porches of saloons and businesses and followed them to the livery, where Roxy opened a big sackful of mail she had collected and began calling out names. Next to whiskey, mail from home was the biggest attraction in town.

When the mail was distributed and the crowds moseyed on back to the saloons, Ki helped unhitch the team of horses while Jessie bargained with the liveryman for a fresh team to be ready to go first thing in the morning.

"A hundred dollars a horse seems like robbery to me," Jessie fumed.

The liveryman smiled, showing missing teeth. "Hell, I'm giving you fifty each for your horses, so you're only paying three hundred dollars' out-of-pocket expenses altogether. Something tells me you can well afford that, miss."

Jessie knew when she was bested. The liveryman was going to make a huge profit off her and there was no help for that. It was a long road back and trouble was coming. Besides, the horses she was bargaining for were superior to those she was trading in.

"All right," she said. "But I'll expect to have them ready at dawn."

"What about passengers? You ain't going to get any at that hour. They'll wait for the Sierra stage that is due in tomorrow morning."

"We don't need passengers," Jessie said, paying the man and hurrying after Ki, Roxy, and Billy.

Billy was hurting. He complained of severe headaches and there was little doubt in Jessie's mind that at least two of his ribs were broken. Jessie stepped in beside him and said, "Here, throw your other arm over my shoulder and Roxy and I can almost carry you to a bed."

"The devil with that! We're getting rid of this damn payroll as fast as we can. Just down the street a ways is the Jumbo Mining Company offices, and the sooner we turn their twelve thousand dollars over to them and get a receipt, the better I'll feel."

"But that's only half the job. We have to deliver the gold back to Reno."

"I know," Billy said. "And I been thinking about that. The gold might be worth a lot more than twelve thousand dollars. Could be that Lee Ford and his men have decided to wait for us and strike somewhere on the return trip."

"I'd be willing to bet they have," Jessie said as they entered the Jumbo Mining Company offices right as the manager was closing.

Jessie introduced herself and, when Ki placed the strongbox full of payroll money down, she said, "We'll want a receipt, of course."

"Of course," the manager said. He was a round-faced man in his thirties who wore a wedding band and a broad smile. "Just as soon as I have a chance to count it."

"Will that take long?" Billy groaned. "My ribs are on fire and we all wanted to send a telegram off this evening."

The man looked at his pocket watch. "I'm afraid you'll have to wait until eight o'clock tomorrow morning. Telegraph office closes same time I do."

Jessie frowned. "We'd like to leave with the bullion at dawn."

"I can have it ready," the man said. "Tell me what time you need it."

"Five o'clock."

The manager sighed. He was no longer smiling. "All right. Do you want the receipt then too, or do you want to wait for it now?"

"We'll get it in the morning along with the bullion," Jessie decided, taking one look at the pain etched across Billy's face. It was clear that he was in need of rest and a doctor's attention.

"Very well. Please lock the door on your way out. This is a lot of money and I'll take no chances."

"Thanks," Jessie said, "for helping us get an early start tomorrow morning. I know it will be quite an inconvenience."

"Never mind that. We are a full week late in meeting our payroll, and if something had happened to this money we'd have had a miners' riot on our hands and a strike as well. I'm just grateful that you weren't robbed."

They locked the door on their way out and headed for the best hotel in town. They would need adjoining rooms, preferably with a connecting door between them so that, in case of trouble, they could fight together. And there was also the matter of Roxy and Ki to consider. They might want to get together sometime in the deep of the night.

Jessie smiled. If that happened, she could play nurse to Billy Bonaday in order to distract the young man should he awaken.

Jessie awoke just before dawn and then awakened Ki and the others. She had heard Roxy leave her room in the night and then return just a short time earlier. But there was no evidence they had made love from the way they both prepared for the day ahead. Roxy seemed a little flushed in the cheeks, but Ki showed no signs of fatigue from the night he had enjoyed making love.

"How are you feeling, Billy?"

"Better," he said. "I'll stretch out in the coach and keep a shotgun and my sixgun loaded and ready. If anyone should stop us, when they open the door they'll wish they had never got out of their bedroll this morning."

Jessie nodded. "Ki, you'll have to drive. I'll ride shotgun. There isn't any choice."

"I should ride shotgun," Roxy said.

"I'm sorry, but I'm a better shot than you are and I want to take care of Ki."

Roxy wasn't pleased. "Well, so do I!"

"I knew him first," Jessie said, ending the discussion. "Let's get out of here. Ki, you and Billy go get the coach while Roxy and I are taking care of business at the Jumbo Mining Company offices. When the bullion is ready to be loaded, I'll step outside to see that everything looks clear. If it does, I'll take my hat off and wave it. That will be the signal for you to drive the coach on down and stop by the door. It ought not to take more than two or three minutes to load the bullion. We'll be out of here before the sun has left the horizon."

And that was how it went. Within forty minutes, Jessie was waving her hat and Ki was helping Billy into the coach with his shotgun cocked and ready. If Lee Ford and his men were in town, this might be their best chance to strike.

Ki started to climb up into the driver's seat, but Austin Higby's voice stopped him. "I had a hunch you folks would be leaving mighty damned early," he said. "If you give me free passage back to Carson City, I'll do the driving."

Ki hesitated. "Maybe it would be better if you took the Sierra stage back. This could be rough."

"In that case, you'll need a real reinsman up there in the driver's box. A man who can handle the lines with a woman's delicate touch and use a whip like Satan himself. No offense, Ki, but if things get dicey out there and you have to make a run for it, one little mistake and you could roll this Concord. Kill everyone in or on top of it. Why take the chance?"

Ki nodded. "All right. It's your neck, and you've been warned. I'm sure we can do better than give you a free fare back."

"We can talk about that later," Higby said, climbing up to the driver's seat. "Get on up here and keep your eyes peeled for ambushers."

Ki swung the door closed behind Billy and climbed up in the box. He watched Austin Higby take the reins expertly and start the coach down the street toward the Jumbo Mining Company. Ki could feel his heartbeat quicken. It seemed to him that, if there was to be an attack, it might very well come the moment that they started to load the gold into the coach.

The coach stopped right outside the office, and Jessie emerged carrying a small but obviously heavy crate. Roxy was right behind her, and next came the mining-company manager. Ki jumped down and helped them. He half expected the roar of an outlaw's gun.

"If you see anything moving in the shadows," he called softly up to Higby, "anything at all, let me know."

"I sure as the devil will!"

In minutes they had the boxes of bullion packed on the stagecoach floor. Roxy jumped in beside her brother and slammed the door. Ki helped Jessie up onto the driver's seat and then he nimbly climbed up onto the roof. There was a Winchester rifle beside him, but it was his bow and arrow that he took into his hands as Higby snapped the whip and the stage shot out of Candelaria. Only then did Ki breathe easily again. Their coach barreled up and over a ridge just as the sun was topping the horizon. It glowed blood-red and the earth seemed hushed as if waiting for a calamity.

Ki sat cross-legged on the roof of the coach and now he slowly revolved in a complete circle. Dark shadows were reluctantly giving way to sunlight. Ki saw nothing but mining claims and prospectors' camps dotting the hills and desert floor. Their small mounds of tailings made it all look like a thriving colony of prairie dogs.

He returned his attention to the north. When would the attack come? Ki strained to see beyond the range of human vision. This land was rough and hilly. Their enemies could be just ahead. Anywhere.

Austin Higby glanced sideways at Ki. He looked damned unhappy. "You and the Bonaday girl sweet on each other?"

"Why do you ask?"

The man shrugged. "I'm sorry. None of my business."

Ki relaxed a little. This man was risking his life to help them. The question was out of line but, given the circumstances, Ki decided to make an allowance. "Roxy is a fine girl. She has made a few mistakes. Namely, trusting that Orin Grayson was an honorable man when he falsely promised to help Dan Bonaday salvage something of this company."

"Dan Bonaday never had a chance."

"What do you mean by that?" Jessie asked.

The driver just shrugged. "You can't win against a stacked deck. You shouldn't even try."

Jessie frowned. "You seem to know a lot about things. Why?"

Higby kept his eyes on the road ahead. "I just learned a long time ago that the little guys like Dan and me, well, we either get smart and join the winners of this world, or we let them crush us."

174

"I don't think I like your attitude," Jessie said angrily. "The 'little guys,' as you call them, are the ones who have to fight the hardest. If they persevere long enough and hard enough, they can win, too."

"Not against a stacked deck," Higby said, his face deeply troubled. "I sure wish that . . ."

"Wish what?" Ki asked expectantly.

"Nothing. Not a damn thing, mister. I just forgot my good sense for a minute and—" He clamped his mouth shut when he saw the Sierra stage suddenly emerge. Higby recognized the driver and the shotgun. It was too late to switch horses in midstream now. He had to go through with this or they'd kill him, too.

"How are you going to play this?" Jessie asked the man beside him as she checked to make sure that the shotgun was ready. Beside her, Ki notched an arrow into his bow.

Higby was slow in answering. He swallowed and said, "There's just two of them, the shotgun guard and the driver, and they got as much right to this road as we have. I'm fixin' to do nothing but sail on by them. But . . . well, no matter what, I wish you luck."

Austin Higby waited until the coaches were just twenty yards apart and thundering toward each other. Suddenly, he pulled hard on the lines and sent the lead horses into a sharp turn. The wheel horses tried to follow, but the Concord coach went into a skid and hit the exact rock that Higby had aimed for. The oaken spokes of the right back wheel shattered, and the Concord crashed over on its side with the sickening sound of splintering wood and twisting metal.

Jessie cried out as she felt herself being hurled into the sky. Beside her, Ki was launched off the stagecoach, too. He heard a tremendous crack as the Concord coach broke apart. A scream filled the air, and then Ki hit a boulder and the world went blank.

He awoke less than a minute later with blood trickling down his face. He tried to see, but everything was in doubles. "Jessie!" he shouted groggily. "Jessie!"

"Get him!" someone yelled, and before Ki could clear the fog and pain from his mind, three men were pinning him down. One punched him in the jaw and Ki sagged as if unconscious. He had to clear the cobwebs from his brain if he was to be of any help.

"Get the women and the blankets!" someone yelled. "The bullion can wait until Ford and his men come. Let's take our pleasure with the women before any more men arrive!"

Ki heard Roxy yell. He felt two of the men leave him and heard the third one cuss. The man punched Ki once more as if to insure that he was unconscious and no threat. "Goddamn it," he bellowed, "we drawed for them women and I got the Bonaday girl first! Get outa my way!"

Ki opened his eyes to see Jessie and Roxy being hauled over to the blankets. Both of them were still too dazed to fight. Ki guessed that Billy was still in the ruined coach, maybe killed in the crash.

Austin Higby stood back from the other men. His face was skinned up, his pants torn away, and his knees were bloody where he had landed on them. "Now wait a minute, boys!" he said. "Nobody said anything about raping women!"

"Aw, shut up!" an outlaw yelled, knocking Higby aside as he fumbled for his belt. "You're just mad because you're gonna be last in line."

Higby stumbled back, his face a mask of revulsion. He had killed men, but never women. He had beaten men, but he had never struck a woman nor raped one, and that was the single thing that he was proudest of. But now, if he was a part of this and didn't stop these animals, he would be just as guilty as they were.

He staggered into the sagebrush and grabbed a shotgun that someone had dropped in the excitement. "Hold it!" he bellowed, raising the gun and pointing it at the knot of men. "Let them girls go and get back away from them, or so help me God I will kill the first man jack of you who touches them again!"

The outlaws spun around. They were armed men and dangerous. There were ten of them, and there was no way that Higby could stop them from having their way with the women. The problem was, Higby held a double-barreled shotgun in his fists, and there was also no way that he could fail to take at least two of them along with him to hell.

"Are you crazy!" Frank screamed.

Higby took a step back. He saw the outlaws start to fan out and knew that he could not stop them. They would get far enough apart that their chances of surviving were increased. "Now listen," he said, "raping and killing women is no damned good. Let's take the bullion, all of it, and ride out now! Don't you see that we'll get bigger shares? We can be in California and—"

"You're a fool!" Frank hissed. "We'd never make it over the Sierras. Ford and his men would catch us in this coach and—"

"But we could cut the traces off both teams and go," Higby argued, almost pleading now. "We could scatter, too. They'd never catch us and—"

"Put it down, Higby! By God, this is your last chance. You can't win."

"Let the women go!" Higby roared.

Frank raised his hands and then made a sideways pushing motion that further widened the line of outlaws. "You lived like a fool," he whispered. "And you are going to die like a fool."

Austin Higby pulled the trigger and saw Frank lift off his feet and blast over backward. He swung the shotgun and killed another man, suddenly understanding that he had at least a slim chance to live. An instant before firing he had seen Ki and both women pull weapons, and as he fell he reached for his sidearm. Another shotgun blast filled the air as Billy Bonaday leapt out of the coach and unleashed two volleys down the line of men. They went flying like bowling pins.

The gunfire died as suddenly as it had started. Ki stood

up, walked over to Jessie and Roxy, and put his arm around them. Billy hobbled over to join them.

Jessie turned and walked over to Austin Higby, who was holding his bloodied shoulder. She gently pulled back his shirt and studied the wound. "You're going to live, Austin. But you were in cahoots with them all along, weren't you?"

"Yeah. I make no excuses for it."

Jessie looked up into his face. "None are necessary. When it came right down to things, you chose honor and courage. You saved our lives, Austin. Help us the rest of the way out of this and you've got a job and friends as long as you live."

"You mean you'd not see to it that I went to prison?"

"How much do you know about Orin Grayson and the three Sacramento men who are named Warner, Wilkins and Heath?"

"I know most all of it. And I'd testify in court."

Jessie nodded. "What's going to happen next?"

Higby took a deep breath. "Any time within the next half hour, Lee Ford and the rest of his men are going to come riding over a hill expecting to find things just as they are, only with them alive and in control. Did you know that right after we pulled out, they was fixin' to rob the Jumbo Mining Company of that payroll you brought in?"

"I had a feeling they might. And then I expect they were going to put it right back on this stage with the bullion and take it back into Candelaria, where no one would ever think to look for it."

"That's right, miss. Next day or two, they would ship it all back to Reno on this very same stage and no one would be the wiser."

"Pretty smart," Jessie admitted. "But I think it's time we outsmarted Ford. Let's hide the dead in the overturned Bonaday stage and all of us get inside this undamaged one and go meet Ford."

Austin Higby grinned. "When he and his boys see me

178

driving back to Candelaria, they'll just think everything went as smooth as could be."

"That's right. Imagine their surprise."

Chapter 16

Ki had changed into one of the dead outlaws' coat and hat. Now, as Lee Ford and the last of his men came galloping up, he left the shotgun in the boot of the Sierra stagecoach. To pick up the weapon would be to warn Ford something was amiss.

Ki glanced sideways at Austin Higby, who was hatless and thus easily recognizable by Ford and his men. "Just take it easy," Ki said as he palmed a *shuriken* star blade and tugged the battered Stetson down low to cover his face. "With luck, there won't be a shot fired."

Austin Higby nodded. When Ford and his outlaws reined their sweating horses in and stopped the coach, Lee Ford shouted, "Any hitches?"

"Nary a one!"

Ford grinned broadly. His round face with its many chins ducked up and down. "We got the Jumbo Mine payroll slick as could be! Twelve thousand dollars in addition to the bullion you're carrying!"

Higby laughed. "Biggest haul ever made in Nevada."

"Big enough to make us all a whole lot better off. And ruin the goddamn Bonaday Stage Line. Where are they, anyway?"

Higby jerked a thumb over his shoulder. "Back over that hill yonder. Coach all smashed to hell."

"And them pretty women?" a mounted outlaw asked "Where are they?"

"Dead." Higby shook his head sadly. "It was terrible th way that coach splintered up. All aboard were killed in th crash."

"Damn! Them women was beautiful!"

Ford glanced sideways at the rider. "Think, man! W got us a huge chunk of money and gold. You complaining Hell, your share alone will buy you enough women work you to death."

The outlaws snickered and the complainer clamped h mouth shut.

"Why don't you load the payroll before somebod comes along and sees this big powwow," Higby suggested nervously looking toward Candelaria.

Ford nodded in agreement. He ordered the transfe Two hard-looking outlaws dismounted, carrying saddle bags bulging with twelve thousand dollars in cash. K steeled himself. When the outlaws threw open the coac door to stare into the guns of Jessie, Billy, and Roxy, the jumped back and threw up their hands.

"What—" Lee Ford's hand scratched for his gun.

"Freeze!" Ki yelled in warning as Billy jumped out wit the shotgun trained on them.

They all froze except for Lee Ford, who went for hi sixgun. Ki's wrist snapped forward whiplike, and the *shur iken* star blade sliced through the air and caught Ford in th throat. The man choked, toppled from his horse, and die most unpleasantly.

The sight of the dead man with his spastic hands claw ing at his severed jugular totally unnerved the outlaws They threw up their hands in a panic. It was easy to disarr and tie them. And it was going to be even easier gettin them and the Jumbo Mining Company payroll back Candelaria.

Ki had a strong hunch that the Jumbo miners woul make sure justice was swiftly served.

• • •

They returned three days later to Reno. They trudged over to Sheriff Colton's office and Austin Higby spelled out the story once, then once again to Judge Heath, who reluctantly wrote out a warrant for the arrest of Orin Grayson.

Jessie studied the warrant and then waved it until the ink was dry. "You can write out your own resignation now—or after the truth comes out in a trial. Take your pick."

The judge did not hesitate and his pen scratched out the termination of his own unethical career.

Jessie took both papers and gave them to the sheriff. "The night you stepped out of the jail and left Ki to be burned to death I was sure you were as crooked as Judge Heath. I found out I was wrong when I checked with the doctor and discovered that your wife really did have a very grave fever and illness. How is she now?"

Colton shook his head and his eyes grew misty. "She lied, Miss Starbuck. We buried her last week. It's hard on me, but it's even worse on my little girl."

Roxy stepped forward and touched his arm. "I'm so sorry. When this is over, can I help by being your friend?"

The sheriff looked right into her eyes. "My wife always said you were a good woman. You grew up together and she liked you very much. She said you just took a wrong path for a while, but that you would see the light of truth come shining through again."

Roxy swallowed and seemed to grow a little taller. "I have many faults. I guess you know about—"

"Miss Roxy," Sheriff Colton said, "I know and I don't give a damn. When this is over, I want you and my little girl to get better acquainted."

Jessie stepped away, and Ki went with her. He had told Roxy again on their trip back to Reno that he would be leaving within a few days. He was happy that she had accepted that fact and was out to become the sheriff's friend, and probably his new wife someday. It showed Roxy's growing confidence and strength. Maybe now Billy was also ready to be a man. He had certainly proven himself on the road to Candelaria.

"What about the sheriff?" Austin Higby asked, stepping up beside them and checking his sixgun. "Aren't you going to wait for him to serve that arrest warrant?"

"No," Ki said. "And this time, I'll have to order you to stay away until this is finished."

Higby slowed his pace, but they still heard him clearly. "Orin Grayson seems like the kind of man who has never held a gun in his life. Don't you believe it. He has a hideout gun behind his belt over his backbone and maybe a derringer someplace else. Watch him—he's deadly if he catches you by surprise."

"Thanks," Jessie said as she and Ki moved on to the Sierra stageyards.

When they walked into the office, Orin Grayson was talking to another man. He took one look at Jessie and Ki, spun on his heels, and darted out the back door. Ki went after him in a rush.

They crossed the yard, running past startled employees. One tried to stop Ki, but found himself flat on his back and stunned for his effort. Another reached up into a stage coach he had been polishing and grabbed for a shotgun. Jessie's bullet pinned the man to the coach, quaking in fear.

Ki was closing on Grayson. They were running down a small street and people were coming out of their yards to stare after they passed. Grayson drew a gun and fired, but he missed badly and kept on running. Ki tugged at the bowknot of his *surushin*, and the rope that bound his narrow waist came loose at a touch. He whirled it completely around three times before he released the six-foot rope with its leather-covered steel balls. The *surushin* whirled ominously toward Grayson and caught him around the knees. It pinned his legs together and dropped him to the dirt. Ki could just as easily have sent it to choke Grayson to death, but he chose not to, for he preferred the man alive.

Grayson crashed to the street and cursed. He grabbed futilely at the *surushin* and then rolled onto his back and fired at the onrushing samurai.

184

Ki dodged sideways and his hand plucked a star blade from his vest. As Grayson started to pull the trigger again, the star blade leapt from Ki's hand and caught Grayson in the forearm. It severed his coat sleeve and the gun dropped as Grayson roared in pain.

"I'm bleeding to death!" he screamed.

Ki stood over the man and folded his arms together. "Your legs are bound and you cannot move. You will bleed to death unless you tell me and these people that it was you who murdered your accountant, Peter Bakemore. You murdered him and sabotaged the Bonaday Stage Line. Is this the truth?"

Grayson was sobbing. He had every right to be upset, for Ki knew that his *shuriken* blade had severed an artery and the man really was bleeding to death.

"Help me! Someone help me!"

"I am the only one capable of saving your life now," Ki told him impassively. "But first, you must admit the truth to everyone."

"All right! I murdered Pete Bakemore and had a part in the Bonaday Stage Line being robbed and sabotaged! Now, please, help me!"

Ki looked around at the people. "You all heard that?"

They nodded grimly. Mothers hid their children's faces from the sight of so much blood.

"It is not necessary for this murderer to repeat the admission of his crimes?"

"For God's sake, save him!" an old woman begged.

"He's getting weaker every second!"

Ki knelt beside Orin Grayson. He pulled out his *tanto* knife and someone screamed, probably assuming he was a murdering heathen about to slit Grayson's throat. Instead, Ki slit the state assemblyman's coat sleeve and rolled it up to the elbow. He yanked the wicked star blade out of the flesh. Grayson fainted just as Jessie arrived.

"Is he dead?" she asked.

"No." Ki found the pressure point on Grayson's muscular arm. He applied his thumb to that spot and the bleeding

185

stopped almost instantly. Jessie took the *tanto* blade and cut the sleeve away completely, using it as a tourniquet. With a second strip of Grayson's coat they bound his arm, and Ki helped the man up and removed the *surushin* binding his knees. He prodded Grayson toward the sheriff and watched him take the wounded man to the doctor's office.

"He confessed," Ki said. "In front of this whole streetful of people, he admitted to the murder of Peter Bakemore and to sabotage."

"He might hang," Jessie said, remembering the poor accountant she had promised a job, "and it would serve him right."

"Don't count on it. Poor men hang; rich and important ones often find a way to save their skins."

"I suppose that's true. But before this is over, he's going to tell the jury everything, including the identities and roles of those Sacramento financiers. They will also be looking at stiff prison sentences."

"So it's over," Ki said with a nod of his head.

"Yes, for us it is." Jessie was glad. "I think it's time we got back to Texas and the Circle Star."

"I agree." Ki could not suppress a grin. "But if it's all right with you, let's go by train."

Watch for

LONE STAR AND THE TWO GUN KID

fifty-fourth novel in the
exciting LONE STAR series from Jove

and

LONGARM AND THE LONE STAR MISSION

the next giant LONGARM
adventure featuring the LONE STAR duo

coming in February!